The Appala

Books in the Choice Adventures series

J
F
Pet

The Appalachian Ambush

Randy Petersen

994

Tyndale House Publishers, Inc.
Wheaton, Illinois

Copyright © 1994 by The Livingstone Corporation
All rights reserved

Cover Illustration copyright © 1994 by John Walker

Library of Congress Catalog Card Number

Petersen, Randy.
  The Appalachian ambush / Randy Petersen.
    p.   cm. — (Choice adventures ; #15)
  Summary: The reader is asked to make choices which will determine the
outcome of a hiking trip adventure for a group of Christian friends on the
Appalachian Trail.
  ISBN 0-8423-5133-7
  1. Plot-your-own stories. [1. Hiking—Fiction. 2. Appalachian
Trail—Fiction. 3. Christian life—Fiction. 4. Plot-your-own stories.]
I. Title. II. Series.
PZ7.P44199Ap 1994
[Fic]—dc20   93-40183

Printed in the United States of America

99 98 97 96 95 94
 9   8   7   6   5   4   3   2   1

My feet itch!"

Chris Martin said this out loud, but he knew there was no one to hear him. His feet were not used to the strong leather hiking boots. He wished he could just kick off his shoes, but that wasn't so easy. The boot laced all the way up his ankle. He'd have to untie his double knot and then pull the laces out of five hooks and five holes on each side. Then he'd just have to put it all back on for his walk back to camp. And by then it might be dark.

How did he get himself into these things? His best friend Willy had talked him into this hiking trip.

"It'll be fun," Willy had said. *Right.* "It'll be an adventure," Willy had said.

Chris had already had plenty of adventures with Willy and his other friends. When Chris, Willy, Sam, Pete, and the others got together, things happened. They called their group the Ringers, from the bell in the tower of Capitol Community Church, where they all attended. Pastor Whitehead had recruited them to ring that bell every Sunday.

Sundown happened fast in the mountains. A few moments ago it was a sunny afternoon. But now the sun was calling it a day. Bright blue turned to dusky gray. Chris figured he'd have to hustle to join the others while he could still follow the trail.

But his feet itched.

2

He sat down and tried to scratch them through the leather of the boots. It was hopeless. As he stood up again, he realized that he had been sitting in some damp soil. The moisture was seeping through his jeans.

"Great!" he said. "Now I have itchy feet and a soggy behind! What's next? Poison ivy?" The thought worried him, but he checked his surroundings and found none of the sinister leaves that would spell trouble.

Why hadn't he stayed in the camp? He could have his shoes off and be warming them by a fire. But no—he had to volunteer to scout out the path ahead.

It was Willy who had prodded him. "Don't be a wimp. Do it. It's not hard." It was the same way he had convinced him to go on this trip in the first place. Willy's older brother, Clarence—everybody called him Zeke—was taking Willy on this hiking trip on the Appalachian Trail. Willy asked if the Ringers could go along. Sam and Pete jumped at the chance, but Chris held back.

"Don't be a lemonhead," Willy had said. "It'll be fun."

Lemonhead? That was a term Willy and Chris had made up for a coward, a sissy, a chicken. If there was one thing Chris was *not,* it was a lemonhead. He would do just about anything on a dare. The other Ringers looked up to him as a leader, in a way. But that was back home. He really didn't know his way around the woods.

He had walked along the trail for exactly a half hour, timed on his digital wristwatch, a favorite possession. Finding no better place to camp than where the rest of the guys were, he headed back, itchy feet and all. He was going slower on the trip back, but he figured he had to be close to camp. As it got darker, it was harder to follow the trail, but he was managing.

Then he heard a growl.

Must be something I ate, he thought jokingly, but he looked around cautiously.

He heard it again, louder, closer. Willy had told him there were bears in these woods. Sometimes they came out at night. That's what Willy said, and he had gone hiking with his brother lots of times. "If you hear a bear in the bushes . . . ," Willy had told him.

There was something moving in the bushes! Chris tried to remember what Willy had said. "If you hear a bear . . ." What was it? He stepped toward the sound to get a closer look, and he thought he saw a large dark shape in the shadows. "If you hear a bear in the bushes . . ." *Think, Chris, think!*

". . .be absolutely still." That's what Willy had told him. Maybe the bear will go away.

Another growl.

What else had Willy said? "If the bear comes toward you and growls, growl back. If it thinks you're another bear, it will leave you alone."

The growl got louder. It seemed just a few feet away. Chris growled back.

Grrrrr! went the sound, again.

Chris clenched his teeth and went "Grrrrr!" He matched the sound as well as he could.

There was silence for a moment. Then, *GRRRRRR!*

Chris shivered when he heard it. *"GRRRRRR!"* he growled back.

4

Almost before he could catch his breath, a huge growl ripped through the woods: *GRRRRRRRRRRRRRRRRRR!*

Turn to page 64.

Willy felt he was probably very close to the shelter. So he could probably find his own way back. No need for the embarrassment of admitting he was lost.

He devised a plan. He would walk five hundred paces in one direction. If he didn't see anything familiar by then, he would turn right and walk another five hundred paces. Then he would turn right for another five hundred, and so on.

The journey began. Five hundred paces was longer than Willy thought, especially in the woods. It took several minutes to complete the first leg of his walk. Still he saw nothing familiar, so he turned right and walked.

Willy knew the sun was going down. He figured he had another half hour of sunlight. As he paced, he thought through his plans. *What if I don't get back? Will they come looking? I guess I'll have to call. But what if it's too late?*

Another five hundred paces and the camp was still not in sight. He turned right again.

"Willy!"

Willy didn't recognize the voice behind him. He whirled around and saw a tall man dressed entirely in black. The man was about thirty paces away.

Willy squinted to see the man's face, but couldn't. "Who are you?" Willy asked.

The man laughed lightly. "A stranger," he said.

6

Willy could now see the stranger had a backpack and knit cap. He had a black beard and mustache, but Willy could see a smile.

"How do you know my name?" Willy asked.

"I hear things," the man said in a gentle voice. "I've been to your camp. Your friends are beginning to worry."

"Are they?" Willy replied, trying to seem like an experienced hiker. "Well, I'm about to head back there. Just picking up some firewood."

The man's smile vanished, and he seemed to stare right through Willy. "Are you lost?"

"W-well, not r-really," Willy stammered. "Like I said, we needed some firewood, so I came out here to get some. It's just taking longer than I thought."

"Are you lost?" the man repeated in a more serious tone. "I can show you the way back."

Who was this man? Why did he care about Willy being lost? All sorts of things ran through Willy's mind. *Do not trust strangers! Do not admit your problems! Whatever you do, ABC—always be cool!*

"If you are lost, I can show you the way back. Are you lost?"

CHOICE →

If Willy admits he is lost, turn to page 36.

If Willy doesn't admit he's lost, turn to page 74.

Let's get out of here," Pete answered. Very quietly the two boys crawled back to the clearing and sat by the place where their campfire had been. They could still feel the warmth of the dying coals and smell the aroma of burning wood.

"So," Sam repeated, still quietly, but no longer in a whisper, "what should we do?"

"Nothing," said Pete.

"What do you mean?"

"Nothing. Zero. Nada. Nil. We go back to sleep and forget it happened."

Sam couldn't believe what he was hearing. If anything, he expected Pete to want to investigate this since Pete's dad worked for the FBI.

"But you heard them! They're planning something *very, very* bad!" Sam pleaded.

"What are they planning?" Pete asked.

"Something *very, very* bad," Sam repeated. "Naughty. Evil. Wicked. Wrong. *You* heard them."

"The thing is, we don't have any idea what they're talking about. And it's none of our business."

Sam was still worried. "But what if it's a crime or something?"

"Then it would be dangerous for us to get involved, wouldn't it?" Pete seemed to have an answer for everything.

8

"Look, we're out here in the middle of nowhere. If we did try to go for help, where would we go? By the time we got to the authorities, those people would be long gone. It's probably just a prank of some kind. College kids."

Sam wasn't convinced. "But what if they find us here?"

"Look, Sam, why would they be sitting in the dark and talking? Because they didn't want to be found. Why would they want to find anyone else?"

"If they're terrorists," Sam suggested, "they might need hostages."

"OK, Sam, maybe they'll take us all hostage. But if they want to do that, they'll do that, even if we run away. We have nowhere to run. They know where this trail goes as well as we do."

"So we sit and do nothing?"

Pete smiled. "We sleep and do nothing. I'm sure there's an innocent explanation for those people. Let's just go back to bed."

Sam reluctantly went back to bed, but he couldn't go back to sleep. He was busy imagining all the terrible things that might happen. He listened for the sounds of terrorists storming their shelter, but the sounds never came.

Finally, slowly, Sam gave in to his tiredness, and sleep overcame him.

Turn to page 67.

Though it was hard to admit it, Chris realized that Zeke was right. Right now, the best thing for Sam and everyone else was just to head home.

"All right, Zeke," Chris said finally. "Let's go."

As Zeke had said, it was about an hour to the place where a road crossed through the mountains. At that point the hikers left the trail and took the road into town.

Meanwhile, the afternoon stretched out before Jill, Jim, and Tina as they sat at the Miller Memorial. There was a plaque there about Colonel Timothy Miller, the Revolutionary War hero, who gave Millersburg its name and actually designed most of its streets. On the metal plaque was a picture of Miller, in profile. For years kids had been rubbing the nose of this portrait, so now it was a bright gold color, while the rest of the plaque had tarnished. Jill stood there, rubbing Miller's nose and thinking.

"I just had an idea," she said. "I'm not really crazy about doing this whole woods thing. I mean, there are little animals and insects, and bushes that'll scratch you, and poison ivy. What if we just hiked around town? This *is* a historic preserve, after all. There are lots of sites that we never pay much attention to."

"I can't believe you're chickening out," said Jim.

Tina rushed to Jill's defense. "She's not chickening out. She just has another idea."

"Well," Jim continued, "I want to hike out in the woods. Let's at least go to the water tower and see what's out there."

"What do you say, Tina?" asked Jill. "You seem to have the deciding vote."

Hmmm, Tina thought, taking a few paces. She put her fingers on the plaque and rubbed a little as the others awaited her decision.

CHOICE ⇒

If they decide to hike through town, turn to page 57.

If they decide to hike through the woods, turn to page 93.

Pete decided to speak up. "I agree with Chris. Let's get the tents up and get out of the rain. Sam really needs a break."

Sam, in pain, nodded.

Zeke looked at his "mutineers" and settled his gaze on his brother, Willy.

"Hate to say it, Zeke, but I'm with them," Willy said.

Zeke felt sure this was a bad idea. But he also didn't want to fight with four fourteen-year-olds. And maybe the bad experience would teach them a lesson.

He began to unpack a tent from his backpack, as did Willy and Pete. Each one found an open patch among the trees and laid out his tent, driving stakes into the damp earth and putting up the poles. Finally, they crawled inside their tents to wait out the storm.

It was miserable. The rain seemed to come right through the walls, and Chris and Willy had a stream going right through their tent. The stakes of Sam and Pete's tent came loose, making it fall in on them under the pounding of the rain. Zeke had found higher ground and stayed the driest of them all.

The rain did not let up until midnight. They got little sleep that night.

The next day was even more miserable. Cold and sleepy, the group emerged from soggy sleeping bags, only to be sprinkled on by the water dripping off leaves and

12

branches above them. No matter what they did, they could not get dry. Everything was soaked.

Zeke helped the others pack up their soggy tents, which were much heavier than the day before.

Chris and Pete caught colds that night, and Sam's shoulder bothered him a few more days. They went home two days earlier than planned.

Zeke was tempted to say, "I told you so," but he didn't. He didn't have to.

THE END

If you haven't met the Pressers yet, turn to page 45 and make different choices along the way.

Or, turn to page 141.

ina really didn't want to go traipsing through the woods either, so they decided not to. They figured the cat could find its own way home anyway.

They said good-bye to Mr. Weatherly and walked over to Ninepin Alley, where Jill tried to remember exactly what had gone on there two centuries earlier. Jim got bored and decided to go home early. This "hike through town" idea wasn't working out so well after all.

THE END

To find out what the other Ringers are doing, turn to page 86 and make different choices along the way.

Or, turn to page 141.

14

"TINA!" Jim called. "JILL! TINA! JILL!"

The girls heard the call and came around to the west side of the tower. They saw Kenny hanging from the catwalk, and Jim up there with him.

"GO GET HELP!" Jim called down to them.

"Where?" Jill shouted. "Back through the woods?"

"NO!" Jim yelled. "FOREST CREEK!" He pointed toward the new development.

The girls ran off to get help. They reached a road and flagged down a car, which took them to the fire station.

Jim stayed with Kenny and tried not to move. Every move he made jolted the catwalk, so he stayed perfectly still. "Are you all right, Kenny?" he asked.

"I think I'm losing my grip!" Kenny moaned.

Jim lay down on his stomach, reached over the side, and grabbed Kenny's skinny elbow with both hands. "I've got you," he said. "You can relax a minute."

"No," Kenny whimpered, still clinging to the rail. His fingers were turning white. He began to struggle to keep his hold, and every movement jolted the catwalk. Jim feared that it might all come down.

"Trust me, Kenny," Jim pleaded. "You have to trust me. Stop moving. Relax. I've got you."

"No," the boy repeated, still struggling and starting to cry.

"Listen to me, Kenny. If you don't relax, this whole thing's going to come down, and me with it. You just have to trust me. I care about you, Kenny. Maybe Mom doesn't and Dad doesn't—I don't know—but I care and Jill cares and Tina cares. If I didn't care, would I be here? I could be down there, free and clear. But I care, Kenny. You have to believe that. Hang on to me and stop squirming."

Kenny whimpered, but slowly he stopped squirming. Jim felt the pull on his arms as Kenny relaxed his own grip. "That's good, Kenny. You're going to be all right. Help will come any minute."

The sound of sirens pierced the air, and a fire truck, ambulance, and police car came screeching up to the nearest road. Two firemen hopped out. One of them got into a basket attached to a crane and was raised up in the air until he was under Kenny. Within seconds, Kenny was safe in his arms, and Jim gingerly entered the basket as well.

Jim and Kenny were taken back to the hospital, just in case. Jim explained to the police what had happened and received a severe scolding for going up the tower to begin with.

At first, Kenny wouldn't talk to the firemen, the nurses, the doctors, or anybody. But Tina got him to give his full name, and the nurses managed to locate his mother, who lived in Forest Creek. Just as Kenny had said, she was divorced from his father and had assumed that Kenny was with him.

When Jim's grandfather found out what Jim had done, it took him a while to figure out whether to ground him for taking Kenny up such a dangerous place or to give Jim

16

a hero party for saving Kenny's life. In the end, Jim got neither punishment nor party, but he felt more like a fool than a hero.

Tina made sure to get Kenny's address. The little runaway had really taken to Jim, especially after Jim saved his life. Kenny practically clung to him and wouldn't let go when it came time to say good-bye. Jim promised him they would see him again sometime.

It wasn't the last they would see of the poor, courageous little boy.

THE END

Turn to page 141.

OK," said Chris. "I'm in. What do we do?"

Willy quickly developed a plan as they continued on their walk toward camp. As they neared the clearing, they moved slowly, quietly. Willy had predicted right; Zeke was tending the fire. He had his back toward them as he hunched over the coals. His plaid shirt stretched tight against his broad back. Chris and Willy rustled some branches as they moved around the outskirts of the clearing, but Zeke took no notice. He seemed lost in thought.

Three small tents stood a safe distance from the fire, one for Chris and Willy, one for Pete and Sam, and the third for Zeke. Willy circled to the tent that Pete and Sam had claimed, and Chris scampered quietly behind him.

"Where are they?" Chris whispered. Willy put his finger to his lips, motioning for Chris to be quiet. Then he put his hands together and tilted his head against them, miming sleep. Pete and Sam had been worn out by the day's journey and wanted to sack out.

Inside the tent, Pete was taking the deep breaths of sleep, but Sam was uncomfortable on the hard ground. He usually tossed and turned in his sleep, and his sleeping bag kept him from getting comfortable. He just lay there, listening to Pete breathing.

Sam reached for his walking stick, which was lying

beside him, and ran his fingers over it. Sam's father had given him this right before he left. "Every walker needs a walking stick," his dad had said, "especially a Ramirez." And he handed over this finely polished staff. At about five feet, it was taller than Sam, and it had intricate carvings near the top. It had belonged to Sam's grandfather, Pablo Ramirez, who had roamed the mountains of Mexico for many years. Pablo had carved symbols of his life into this stick, and now Sam tried to read them.

Suddenly, Sam heard something hit the tent. *A pebble? An acorn falling from a tree?*

Then there was another tap against the canvas. *Mutant attack squirrels bombarding me from a treetop?*

Then Sam heard a scratching against the canvas. There was the dim shadow of a paw. Then he heard a low growl. As he fingered the staff, he found the carving of a paw print. Had his grandfather met up with a wolf in his travels?

Sam nudged Pete, who bolted awake. "What! What!" Pete muttered as he reached for his glasses.

"There's something out there," Sam whispered. "Listen."

They both heard another growl, then some panting. "I think it's a wolf," Sam said, "maybe two."

"Let's get Zeke," Pete suggested.

"No," Sam said, grabbing his walking stick. "I can do this."

Sam, son of Juan, son of Pablo, crept out of his tent to do battle. As Sam peered out, he saw Zeke lost in thought, still hunched over the fire. Sam slithered silently, snakelike, along the side of the tent, just around the corner from the threatening beast. He paused a few moments to muster some courage. Then the scratching continued, there was another growl, and Sam leaped into action.

Chris was a few steps behind Willy, laughing hysterically but silently as Willy crouched against the tent, scratching the canvas and growling. Suddenly Sam jumped into view, with his walking stick raised high above his head, "COWABUNGAAAAA!"

Willy looked up in horror, but Sam recognized him too late. The stick was already coming down toward Willy's head. Chris closed his eyes, expecting a terrible injury to his best friend.

It all happened so fast. . . .

As Willy saw it, the stick was a foot away, coming fast, and he was frozen with surprise. Suddenly a hand came out of nowhere to stop it. There was the sharp slap of wood meeting skin, but Willy's head was untouched.

Chris opened his eyes to see Zeke standing between Sam and Willy, holding the staff where he stopped it.

Sam was stunned. "Willy! I'm sorry!" he gasped. "I didn't know."

Willy's heart was pounding. "I'm sorry," he muttered, "I didn't mean—"

Zeke's voice was stern. "All of you! Around the fire! NOW!"

All the boys were still shaking as they sat on the ground in a semicircle around the fire. They all stared at the ground, except for Pete, who looked up at Zeke, who stood on the other side of the flames.

"What was *that?*" Zeke began. "What *was* that? Sam,

20

are you suddenly 'The Exterminator' or something? And Willy, what were you doing behind the tent?"

Chris could tell that Zeke was really angry at his younger brother. Somehow, when it's all in the family, those emotions get even stronger. He was afraid that Zeke would send Willy home, or call off the trip for everybody.

Maybe I should say something, Chris thought. *I was sort of helping Willy. But then it was his idea. And he scared me really bad. Maybe I should let him learn his lesson.*

CHOICE ⇒

If Chris decides to take part of the blame, turn to page 123.

If Chris decides to let Willy take all the heat, turn to page 85.

I don't want any help!" the boy cried. "I just want my blanket!"

Jim let the blanket drop to the ground. "OK, OK," he said. "It's yours. We're leaving." With that, he turned and walked away. Jill followed him quickly.

Tina took a last look at the young runaway. For just a moment the boy looked up, into her eyes. She hoped that he saw warmth there, more warmth than a blanket could ever give him. She hoped that he saw hope in her eyes. Tina did not know what words to say, but her eyes were pouring out a message of concern. *Whatever your problem is,* she wanted to say, *you'll be OK. Reach out for help, please.*

"Come on, Tina!" Jill called, and Tina hurried to join her friends.

They had fun that afternoon, exploring the water tower and climbing its rusty steps. But Tina was still haunted by that vision of the boy who needed help but didn't want it.

She told her grandfather about it that night, and together they decided to call the police. Tina gave a report on the runaway in the woods, and the officer promised to investigate.

Maybe the boy would get some help after all.

22

THE END

If you're curious about what else could have happened on this hike through the woods, turn to page 93 and make different choices along the way.

Or, turn to page 141.

Let's get out of here," Sam whispered.

"Let's go tell Zeke," Pete said. "He'll know what to do."

The boys scampered back to the shelter and woke up their companions.

"What's going on?" Zeke asked.

"There are some terrorists out there," Sam explained. "Pete and I heard them talking."

Chris laughed. "Have you been dreaming again, Sam?"

"No," said Pete. "I heard them, too."

"What did they say?" Zeke asked, still not entirely awake.

"Well," said Sam, trying to remember, "one guy was going to 'take out' some people, and the other was going to 'take out' some other people."

"Sounds like they're planning their prom dates," Chris quipped.

"No, really," Pete said. "This is serious. They said that they wouldn't get caught, and they had someone on the inside. It was like they were spies or something."

"What should we do, Zeke?" asked Sam.

CHOICE ⇒

If Zeke takes it seriously, turn to page 118.

If he ignores it, turn to page 90.

24

Chris stared back at Zeke and said, "Well, you're not much of a leader if you don't have any followers." It was a strong thing to say, but Chris felt strongly about it. He had always seen himself as sort of a leader of the Ringers, and he didn't like the way Zeke came in and took charge. "You don't have the right to tell us what to do," Chris continued. "We want to keep hiking. Right, guys?"

Sam and Pete weren't quite sure what they wanted. Willy wanted to hike, but he didn't like the battle that was brewing between his older brother and his best friend.

Zeke smiled a little. "I don't know how you're getting back to Millersburg, then. It's my car, remember? If I decided to go home tonight, you'd be stuck."

"You wouldn't do that," said Chris.

"And why not?"

"Because you don't have any reason to," Chris answered triumphantly. "If Sam keeps hiking, then there's no reason to cut the trip short. You don't want to stop either."

Zeke nodded toward Sam, who was lying back on the log with his head turned toward them. "But I think Sam wants to go home."

"Let's ask him," Chris said as he turned toward Sam.

"So, Sam," said Willy, who was sitting at Sam's feet, "I guess it's up to you."

"Just leave me here, men. It's no use. I'm done for. Seven-eights dead now."

"Come on, Sam, you can hike," Chris insisted.

"Don't do that to him," said Pete, obviously bothered with this whole argument. "How would you feel if you were in his shoes?"

"Or in my shirt," Sam quipped.

"I think this is getting ridiculous!" Pete went on. "Sam isn't a quitter, but he's hurting real bad. Sure, it would be nice to go on, but it wouldn't be very nice for Sam."

Zeke put his arm up for emphasis. *"Thank* you. Which is exactly why I say we should stop now and go home."

Again, Chris disagreed. "But you don't know Sam like we do, Zeke! It would make him feel worse to make us stop now. That kind of pain—the feeling that you've let down your friends—is worse than any pulled muscle. Right, Sam?"

"Well—"

"I just want to do what's best for you, Sam," said Zeke, walking over to where Sam lay.

Pete stood up quickly. "Hold it a second. Just be quiet." He paced around to gather his thoughts.

Zeke and Chris were both standing, almost like lawyers before a court, each one making his case. Sam, lying down, was like the judge's bench, and Willy, sitting at his feet, was where a witness might be. Now Pete took the judge's spot, standing behind the log, behind Sam, across from Chris and Zeke.

"I don't think either of you wants what's best for Sam," Pete said. "I just think you want to win. Zeke, you're older, and we're really glad that you're here to help us out. Chris, you're our friend, and we like you. You both have good ideas, but now you both want to be the leader—and it's not working. So, let me suggest something. Zeke, you go over there and cool off. Chris, you go over there and cool off. Sam and Willy and I will decide what we want to do. OK?"

Zeke, surprised, put both hands in the air, almost in surrender. "OK. OK," he said, backing away.

Chris went off sulking.

The three others talked briefly and then called Zeke and Chris back. It was Willy who explained their decision. "We want to keep hiking, but to take it easy for the next day or two while Sam's shoulder gets better. So maybe we cover half as much ground, but we stay on the trail. Zeke, do you think we can change our schedule to make that happen?"

Once again, a surprised smile crossed Zeke's lips. They were not doing what he had suggested, but they were being really mature about it, except for Chris. Zeke knew that one reason for hiking trips was exactly this—learning to make decisions. In a way, he was proud of Pete and Sam and his little brother for the way they handled it.

"Yes," he told them. "We can do that."

"So we're going to keep hiking?" asked Chris.

"I guess we are," said Zeke.

Chris grinned. "So I won."

"No," said Pete.

"I think Sam won," said Willy, patting the prone boy on the ankle.

"What did I win?" Sam perked up, though no one paid much attention.

"I think we all won," said Pete. "But one more thing. We've all got to hike together, and we feel there's some bad blood between you, Chris, and you, Zeke. Do you think you could apologize to each other and start fresh?"

"What did I do wrong?" asked Chris.

"It's just a suggestion," said Willy.

"No really," Chris repeated. "What did I do wrong? I believed in something and I said it. Is that wrong?"

"You just didn't seem to be getting along with Zeke very well," Willy explained, almost as if *he* were apologizing. "We just want everyone to like each other."

CHOICE ➤

If Chris and Zeke apologize to each other, turn to page 41.

If they don't, turn to page 96.

28

Meanwhile, back in Millersburg, Jill Martin was feeling sad.

The Ringers (except for Jim) had gone off without her. The camping trip had seemed like a great idea when Willy first mentioned it. But they had gear for only four kids besides Willy's older brother.

Jill could count. This wasn't the first time that those four guys—Willy, Sam, Pete, and Chris (her own cousin!)—had left her out. She knew that they sometimes liked to be with "just the guys," but that bothered her. Why couldn't they accept her as an equal? She was a year younger, but just as smart as they were, and she had more energy than all of them put together!

It might have been different if Jim and Tina Whitehead were around. They were missionary kids who lived with their grandparents in Millersburg. Tina was Jill's age and kind of shy, but Jill liked her. Jim was a year older and pretty nice—for a guy. But the Whiteheads had gone on vacation to see some uncle in Chicago. Who knew when they'd be back?

So there was Jill, stuck in Millersburg. It wasn't even her own hometown! Her parents lived in Washington, D.C., but they had sent her to stay with Aunt June for this summer. They thought she might have more fun hanging around with her cousin Chris and his friends. And it had been fun—sometimes. But now Chris and company were hiking the Appalachians without her. Cousin Bonnie was older and working all the time. Cousin Nancy was only nine, and she still played with dolls. Aunt June got home in time to pop dinner in the microwave—but other than that, Jill was on her own.

So the first day without the Ringers was pretty lonely for Jill. Mostly, she hung out at the Freeze, talking to Betty Metz, the owner, trying to think of new ice cream sundaes to make. Jill even helped Betty put some of their ideas for new creations together and then tested them out. That may not sound so bad, but she ended the day with an awful stomachache.

The next morning, Jill woke up to cousin Nancy tugging on her arm. "It's the phone," Nancy said. "For you."

"I knew it," Jill said to herself as she plodded down the hall. "They're calling from the Appalachians. They need me after all."

But it was a girl's voice on the line. "Jill? It's Tina." The phone line had some static.

"Tina! This is a surprise. Do you miss me?"

"Well, yes," Tina said. "What's cooking?"

Jill sniffed at the air. "I don't know. I don't think anything's cooking."

Tina sighed. "I mean, what's going on?"

"Oh," said Jill, "same old stuff, I guess. Where do you get this 'What's cooking?' line—do they say that in Chicago?"

"Yeah, I guess. My uncle says it a lot."

"So, Tina, how's everything in Chicago?"

There was a brief pause and some more static. "Fine, I guess." Then more static. "Jill, can you hear me OK? This is a really bad connection."

"Yeah, it's OK," Jill answered, "considering you're way out in Chicago."

"But I'm not. I'm home. I just think Grampa needs to get the phone fixed."

Jill smiled for the first time in twenty-four hours. "You're home? But—"

"We got in late last night."

"Well, come on over. We've got a lot of catching up to do."

Tina and Jim both came over and told Jill all about their vacation. And Jill told about the other Ringers going off on their hiking trip, having spent lots of time planning it—but leaving her behind.

"What a bummer to be left behind," said Jim.

"Well," Jill explained, "they only had gear for four kids."

"Still," Jim went on, "they could have figured out—wait a second!" He interrupted himself with a thought that was brilliant—at least in his own mind. "I have an idea. Maybe we could go on our own hiking trip."

"Where?" asked Jill.

"Around town. There's a lot of Millersburg that we haven't really explored."

"Millersburg?" Jill sounded skeptical.

"Sure!" Jim answered. "We don't need to go to the mountains! Our adventure can be right here!"

"And maybe—," Tina began. "No, forget it."

"What?" the others asked.

"Maybe we could even camp out in our backyard."

Jim loved the idea. Jill wasn't so sure.

"I can see it now," Jill said. "The guys come back talking about all the wonders of the wilderness, and we say, 'Big deal! We walked around Millersburg.' I don't think so. Let's just play Pictionary all week."

CHOICE

If they go hiking around town, turn to page 45.

If they do something different, turn to page 70.

Zeke!" Willy called out. "ZEE-EEEK!"

If he were really close, Willy figured, then Zeke would hear him and come to him. No one would have to know Willy was lost at all. Zeke would come out and Willy would say, "I just wanted to show you something."

"Like what?" he would say. And Willy would say, "This firewood—is it all right to burn it?" And Zeke would say, "Of course it is," and Willy could follow him back to camp. No teasing.

Except Zeke might think he was kind of dumb. . . .

"ZEKE! ZEEEE-EEEEEK!"

Willy was getting no reply. The woods were quiet and hushed. He heard a rustle to his left and saw the bushy tail of a squirrel as it scampered away. He heard a flutter above him as a bird took off for another branch. Every sound seemed louder than usual. Willy felt very alone.

What would happen? What if he couldn't find his way back before dark? They would come looking for him, right? But what if they started too late and it got dark? Willy had no idea how far he had run while chasing the deer. Maybe they wouldn't find him. How would he ever find his way back? What if he couldn't?

Then a voice came to him. No, it wasn't a real voice, just a scrap from his memory. A Sunday school class from a couple of years ago. It was the voice of his dear old teacher, Miss Whitehead. *"Why worry when you can pray?"*

Miss Whitehead, who was Jim and Tina's aunt, had died about a year before. It was a great loss for Millersburg, especially for Chris and Willy. But her memory lived on. Often the two boys would remember bits of things she had taught them. And here was one of them: *Why worry when you can pray?*

Willy didn't pray a lot. He was too busy just being a kid. But this was a time when he needed help. He needed to stop worrying and start praying.

"God," he said out loud, "I don't know where I am. Maybe I shouldn't have gone chasing that deer. I don't know. But I'm here now, wherever that is, and I need to get back to camp. Please show me the way."

Willy waited. He wasn't sure what else to say. He wanted a thought, a great idea about what to do, to pop into his head, so he waited.

Nothing.

"Lord, Zeke told me to get firewood and that's what I should've done. . . ." There was nothing but the sound of the woods. In the silence, Willy could hear his own heart pounding.

And then he heard it—a strange voice.

"Willy!"

Willy nearly jumped out of his skin and looked around in every direction. There was Zeke coming toward him.

"Zeke! How long have you been there?"

"A few minutes. I came out to help you gather wood, but then I saw you chasing all over like a crazy man."

"There was a deer. I was chasing it."

"Oh," Zeke laughed, shaking his head. "I couldn't figure that out. So anyway, you were chasing it and I was chasing you, and then you stopped and started praying. That was good. *Good,* dude."

"Yeah, well just don't tell anyone I was scared out of my pants."

Zeke laughed. "Your secret's safe with me."

"So," Willy asked cautiously, "did I do the right things?"

Zeke looked confused.

"For a hiker lost in the woods?"

"Oh yeah, sort of. You called for help, which is good. And then you prayed, which is really good. And best of all, you admitted you should have listened to your brother. That was most excellent."

"Oh, that doesn't count!"

"Sure it does," laughed Zeke. "God and I both heard it."

Willy laughed too. "Now that I've found some firewood," he said, raising the branch in his hand to chest level, "we can get back to camp."

The two Washington boys poked through the woods for some good wood to burn, and they collected a bundle of it. Then they headed back toward the shelter—or so they thought. After a few minutes of walking, Zeke stopped. "Wait a minute," he said thoughtfully. "I thought the shelter was over this rise."

"What do you mean, *you thought?*" A new flash of worry darted through Willy's mind.

"I think we're lost," said Zeke.

35

"You're kidding, right?"

"I wish I were," said Zeke, studying the terrain. "With all that chasing—you chasing the deer, me chasing you—I got turned around. We've been going the wrong way. I have no idea which direction the shelter is."

"What'll we do?"

"Give me a minute," said the older Washington. "Maybe I can figure this out."

"It's getting dark."

"I know! I know! Just give me a minute."

"Uh," Willy suggested quietly, "maybe we should call for help."

"Oh, that'll be great," Zeke crowed. "I'm supposed to know my way around this trail. I'm your guide. If I get lost in the woods, you guys will never listen to me again."

"We really haven't been listening to you much anyway."

"Thanks, Will."

"So how are we going to get back?"

"I'm thinking. I'm thinking."

CHOICE ⇒

If they call for help, turn to page 52.

If they try to find their own way back, turn to page 80.

Yes," Willy finally said. "I am lost. It was that deer. I was chasing it around and it led me—"

"No excuses," the man said sharply. "No excuses are necessary. It does not matter how you got lost. You're lost, and you need to find your way back."

Willy hesitated. "Yeah," he said finally. He was surprised at how much freedom he felt. It was as if there had been some deep secret he was holding, but now he could let it go. He was lost, but now he was headed back to camp.

Or so he hoped.

"Follow me," the man said, turning swiftly and striding away.

Willy hurried after him, but he kept thinking, *Is this right? Should I trust this man? Should I follow him?*

The man remained a safe distance in front of him, but Willy remained alert, ready to run away at any sign of trouble. *Who is this man? Why is he helping me?*

The man stopped suddenly and looked at the base of a tree trunk. Stooping down, he ran his hand over a place where the bark was falling away. Willy stopped too, and watched.

When the stranger stood and resumed walking, Willy was just a few paces behind him. "So," Willy asked, "where are you from?"

"Very near and very far," the man replied. "These mountains are my home."

Willy decided not to try to pin him down on that point, but raised another line of questioning. "Do you have a family?"

The stranger spread his arms wide. "All who walk these woods are my family."

"That's nice," Willy replied, "but really—are you married? Do you have kids?"

"I am married to the wind," the man said, with a glance upward.

"STOP!" Willy said, coming to a standstill. "This is just getting too weird."

The man kept walking. So Willy hurried after him. "Wait a second! Hey, wait up! Look, I'm trying to have a conversation with you, and you're giving me this stuff about being 'married to the wind.' What is that? You asked me to be honest with you, and I was. I'm lost. I need your help. Now I'm asking you to give me a straight answer. Do you have a wife, a family?"

The man stopped and turned so fast that Willy's heart jumped. For a few seconds, Willy had to fight for breath. The man's face looked very serious.

"I did," he said.

"What happened?"

The man pivoted and began walking faster than before. Willy struggled to keep up. "All right," Willy gasped. "You don't want to talk about it. I understand."

They walked a minute in silence before the stranger stopped again. He turned to Willy and pointed to their left.

"Walk one hundred paces in that direction, and you will be there."

Willy saw tears in the man's kind eyes. "I'm sorry I brought that up," Willy said. But he thought for a second, then said. "No, I'm not. I really appreciate all your help, but you've got to open up about these things. If you keep all that pain inside, it'll rot you out. My dad's like that."

There were more tears in the stranger's eyes. Willy wondered if anyone had ever talked to him like this. "We're probably having dinner now," Willy said. "You could join us."

The man shook his head.

"Your wife," Willy said. "Was she beautiful?"

"Like the wind," said the stranger. He seemed to point up and away over Willy's head. Willy turned and looked, and when he turned back, the stranger was gone.

Willy felt a chill. *I hope he's all right,* he thought. *One. Two. Three . . .* He paced his way back to camp.

The others were thrilled to see Willy. They were just planning to go out after him.

"So where's the firewood?" Zeke asked.

Willy looked sheepish. "I left it in the woods. I can go back and get it."

"NO!" they all said. Zeke explained that he had found some himself. And, in fact, a campfire was already raging.

After dinner, Willy asked Zeke to tell more of the legend of the Appalachian Samaritan—where he came from, who he was. Zeke spun the tale of a man who came home from a hiking trip to find his house destroyed by a storm, his wife and children missing. He went back to the

39

mountains, the legend has it, where he helps people in
need.

    Willy kept quiet about his encounter with the man in
black, but he prayed for him that night.

THE END

If you haven't found out who Midnight is, turn to page 28
and make different choices along the way.

Or, turn to page 141.

Sam ran. He heard voices behind him. He felt the heavy pounding of feet as he scrambled up an incline. It was dark, pitch dark, but somehow he knew where he was going. Behind him, the men were getting snagged on bushes and bumping into trees, but Sam was breezing through the woods.

He burst out into the clearing and saw the smoldering ashes of the campfire. He had night vision by now. He could see as if it were day. He saw the three bodies in their sleeping bags in the shelter, and he ran out onto the trail.

But there were more men behind him now, more than four. There were ten or twenty, and they were gaining on him. He ran as hard as he could. He ran and ran and ran and ran and . . .

But they were gaining.

Turn to page 67.

Chris looked at his best friend, Willy. *Yeah, he's right,* Chris thought, but it was still hard to say the words. He wanted this to be a good trip, but somehow Zeke was getting on his nerves. Chris knew he had said some bad things. His attitude was awful. And he felt bad about all that, but it was so hard to apologize. Would the other guys think he was weak if he backed down?

The look on Willy's face—it was a challenge, a dare. Are you going to say you're sorry like you should? Chris wasn't sure.

It was Zeke who stepped forward with an outstretched hand. "Chris, I'm sorry for being disrespectful of your opinion. I want to be friends, OK?"

In an instant, Chris grabbed Zeke's hand and shook it. "No, Zeke, I was wrong. I've had a bad attitude. I'm sorry."

And so the group resumed its journey in good spirits. For the next two days, Sam's backpack was carried by the others, but by then his shoulder had healed enough to carry it himself. Often Zeke and Chris walked together in the front of the line. Their disagreement and apologies seemed to make them better friends. As they walked together, Zeke taught Chris a lot about hiking and camping.

There was lots of laughter on the trail. They talked about the beautiful sights they were seeing, about life back home, about the upcoming school year, about parents and church and girls. Each night, Zeke would write a letter to his girlfriend, Brianna, whom he had met in his botany class at college. Of course he didn't plan to send them—just saved them for hand delivery when he got home.

With three days left on their ten-day trip, they were coming up to another of those roads that crossed the mountains. The boys teased Zeke about running away. "Watch out! He'll slip away in the middle of the night and run home to Brianna."

The truth was that all of them were ready to go home, though no one wanted to admit it. Having gone this far, they didn't want to give up. Yet they were tired. Great trip or not, seven days was a long time. (As Sam put it later, "Seven days of hiking makes one weak.")

They stopped for a lunch break and put down their packs. Zeke sat down with his journal to write another letter to Brianna, but he had left his pen in his pack. "Sam," he said, "could you hand me my pack?"

"No way," said Chris. "Remember what happened the last time Sam tried that. I'll get it for you."

As Chris picked up Zeke's backpack, he noticed a strap that was fraying. "What's this, Zeke?" Chris said in mock horror. "Your backpack is falling apart!"

Willy picked up on it right away. "Those straps are very important, too. They connect the canvas bag to the aluminum frame and distribute the weight of the pack evenly over your back."

"You know, Will," said Chris, as if he were some

talk-show host, "if that strap were to break, I don't think Zeke could go on hiking."

"Right, Chris," Willy agreed. "He'd be risking serious back injury. I think we would have to cut the trip short."

Zeke was laughing through this whole thing. "Well, guys, there is this road we'll reach in about half an hour. We could hike into town and catch a bus to the car."

"And be home by nightfall!" Sam crowed.

"Wait!" Chris said, with the backpack still in his hands. "This strap isn't broken yet. And if we gave up while the strap was still good, then we'd be quitters." He gave the strap a yank. A few more threads tore.

"But on the other hand," Willy continued, "if our equipment wears out, well, there's not much we can do about that now, is there?"

Chris pulled again, and the strap frayed even more.

"Especially," Chris added, "if the strap tore in the normal process of hiking." He put the backpack on and jumped high into the air, coming down with a jolt. The heavy pack pulled more against the strap.

Willy tried to keep a straight face. "You mean normal stuff like jumping up and down a lot?"

"Exactly." And Chris jumped, jolting the pack with each landing, tearing the strap thread by thread.

Finally the strap broke, and the pack sagged against Chris's back. The Ringers gave a mighty cheer.

"Oh, poor Zeke," Chris said. "His pack broke. Now he'll have to go home to Brianna!"

"Come on you geeks," Zeke said as they headed for the road.

44

THE END

To find out what Jill, Tina, and Jim are up to in Millersburg, turn to page 28 and make different choices along the way.

Or, turn to page 141.

Look, Jill," said Tina, "I don't care what we say to the guys when they get back. We're not doing this for them. We're doing this for us. I think it will be fun to hike around town."

"Me too," said Jim. "Come on, Jill, what do you say?"

"Well . . . all right. Let's do it. When do we start?"

"We could start this afternoon," said Jim. "There's that whole wooded area down past the Freeze. I've never been out there, have you?"

Both girls shook their heads.

"So," Jim continued, "let's go there this afternoon. We won't need packs or anything, 'cause we'll be back before dark."

"But we probably need good shoes," Tina piped in. They all looked down at their feet. Jim had old beat-up sneakers, Tina had sandals, and Jill was barefoot. "And wear long pants," she went on, "in case there are branches or bushes or anything."

"Or porcupines," Jill added.

The others looked at her oddly.

"We probably don't have them here," Jill explained. "But Chris read that they sometimes have porcupines on the Appalachian Trail—porkies, they call them. So you're supposed to wear long pants. And if it looks like someone dropped a scrub brush on the trail, just let it be. Especially if it moves."

The others still looked at Jill oddly.

"You know, Jim," said Tina. "I think Jill missed us."

The day had dawned early in the Blue Ridge Mountains. At least it seemed early for Sam. He had been wrestling a vicious wolf in his dreams, and when he woke up, he was worn out. He crawled out of his sleeping bag and joined his friends around the fire.

Pete looked up. "Did you win?"

"Huh?" Sam had no idea what he was talking about.

"You were wrestling somebody last night," Pete said. "When I woke up, you were all twisted in your bedroll. I think you had him pinned."

Sam smiled weakly. "That was no ordinary wrestling match," he boasted. "I was saving Mexico from Ray Lobo, the king of the wolves."

"Oh yeah," Chris said casually as he rinsed off his breakfast plate. "I did that last week."

Willy thought that was really funny, so he was cackling, but Sam was still halfway in his dream. "I'll bet you don't even know where Mexico is," Sam snapped.

"Sure I do," said Chris. He pointed away from the rising sun. "You walk that way until you get to an ocean, then you turn left."

Willy cackled some more, but Sam was not amused. He went back to his tent and picked up his walking stick.

"Breakfast, Sam?" asked Zeke, as he poured some scrambled egg mix onto a skillet.

Sam looked at the so-called eggs suspiciously. "Is it dead?"

"Speak now, Ramirez," Zeke threatened.

Sam held out his plate. "Tell it to be nice to me."

Back in Millersburg, a trio of hikers hit the black asphalt of their familiar streets. They talked and laughed on the way, teasing each other about the "wild animals" they encountered—squirrels and blue jays and four-year-olds on tricycles.

As they passed the Freeze, they peered in the window, looking for Betty, the owner. "I think we need to fuel up for the trip," said Jill.

"Me too," said Jim. "I think a strawberry sundae would keep me strong the rest of the day."

"How about a Triple Chocolate Sundae Supreme?" Jill asked.

"What's that?"

"Just something new that Betty and I made up while you were away," Jill said proudly. "You crumble a chocolate chip cookie on a hot fudge sundae and smother that in M&M's. It's awesome!"

Jim licked his lips. "Let's do it."

Sam kept thinking about his dream, wrestling the wolf, and he wondered what it meant. He walked more slowly when he was deep in thought, so the others were always waiting for Sam to catch up. That bothered them, and they were beginning to get frustrated with Sam.

At lunchtime, they stopped in a small clearing and put down their packs. Zeke was pointing out some of the different trees that surrounded the clearing. He had studied botany in a college class, and he was reviewing his mental notes. Pete was pretty smart and liked learning things, too, so he was right there at Zeke's shoulder, examining leaves and guessing what each tree was. Chris and Willy didn't know much about all that stuff, but they were making a game of it. Sam sat by himself, munching on his lunch.

Bored with the game, Willy walked over to Sam and asked, "What you eating there?"

"Sammmwcchh," Sam muttered with his mouth full.

Zeke, realizing the Ringers shouldn't stop for too long, said, "About fifteen more minutes for lunch, then we'd better hit the trail again. There's a long way to go to get to the shelter tonight, so Sam has the right idea—let's chow down and move out."

"My lunch is still in my pack. It's right behind you," said Chris, pointing to Sam. "Could you hand it over to me?"

Sam reached behind him and tugged at Chris's backpack. "This thing weighs a ton. You didn't have to bring a microwave, you know."

"Well, it's not too heavy for *me*," Chris teased.

"Sam's just worn out from wrestling Ray Ear Lobe," said Willy.

Sam gave an extra pull and hoisted the pack up, handing it to Chris. "No problem," he said. "Just don't bring your bathtub next time."

But as Sam hoisted the pack, he felt a sharp, sudden pain in his shoulder. He winced, but no one noticed.

"I'm stuffed," said Jim Whitehead, walking out of the Freeze. "Let's just go home."

"Wasn't this hike your idea in the first place?" said Tina.

"Yeah," said Jim, running his fingers through his dark hair. "But that was before Triple Chocolate Sundae Surprise."

"Supreme," Jill corrected.

They decided they would waddle into the woods. A half hour later, they sat on the benches by the Colonel Miller Memorial, at the edge of town. "I wonder how the others are doing," said Tina.

The others were doing just fine, except for Sam, whose shoulder was hurting more with every step. He was lagging behind, as before, but the others had grown tired of waiting for him. When Sam finally decided to tell them about his injury, he had to catch up first, and that wasn't easy.

Pete was admiring the greenery along the trail as he walked. Every so often he'd call forward to Zeke, who was leading the way, "Hey, that's a beech, isn't it?"

Then Pete heard footsteps behind him, and the voice of his friend, out of breath, calling, "Wait up, guys!"

Sam looked awful. He had a pained look on his face, and he labored with each step. "Something's wrong with me," Sam said through a grimace.

"He finally admits it!" Willy yelled.

Pete helped Sam take his pack off, and Zeke came back to examine Sam. "I think I broke a fan belt back at lunch," said Sam, pointing to his sore shoulder.

"Why didn't you say something?" the older boy scolded.

"I didn't know how bad it would get."

"Well, you can't carry a pack anymore, that's for sure," said Zeke. "But are you OK just walking?"

50

Sam tried a few steps. "I'd be OK just floating."

Zeke mulled over their situation. At their present pace, they'd make it to the next shelter by sunset, but they had no time to spare. They could stop now and let Sam rest, but then it would be dangerous later on. Or they could press on and hope that Sam would be all right if someone else carried his pack. Zeke voted for pressing on. Pete saw the pain on Sam's face and voted to rest for a while. Sam voted to take a hot bath.

CHOICE

If they press on toward the shelter, turn to page 109.

If they stop for a while, turn to page 86.

Sam sided with Chris. "Look, it isn't like these people are our close personal friends or something. We don't really know them from moss monkeys."

"But they're really nice!" said Pete.

"Yeah," said Willy, "but Sam's right. I say we hike on our own."

So that's what they did. They passed up the invitation to hike with the Pressers, who took off early the next morning. The Ringers hiked alone.

Pete kind of missed Bob's hearty laugh as he walked the trail that day. He decided that he would learn more about deaf kids—maybe learn sign language, maybe try to help someone out.

It was a pretty boring hike the rest of the week.

THE END

A loser week, eh? Turn to page 28 and see what else lay in store for the Ringers.

Or, turn to page 141.

Without warning, Willy threw back his head and yelled,
"HELP!"

"What are you doing?" Zeke asked with a glare.

"You said it was good to call for help when you're
lost," Willy answered. "If it's good for me, it's good for us."

Zeke shook his head and smiled. He showed Willy
how to call out in each direction, not just up into the air.
"Don't just scream at the top of your lungs," he told him.
"That ruins your voice and doesn't go as far anyway.
Scream at the bottom of your lungs."

Suddenly Willy saw a figure through the trees. It was
only about thirty yards away. "Who's that?" asked Willy,
pointing.

"I don't know," Zeke replied, peering intently in that
direction.

"HEY!" Willy called out. The figure waved. Willy waved
back. The figure waved again. Willy waved again.

"HELP!" he called, louder. The figure just kept waving.

"I can't believe this," Willy muttered. "This person
thinks he's in a beauty pageant."

"No," said Zeke, "he's telling us to come to him. Let's go!"

Zeke grabbed the few pieces of firewood he had set
down and took off. Willy was close behind. As they got to
where the figure had been, they lost him.

"That's strange," said Zeke.

"Look!" shouted Willy, pointing to their right.

Through the trees, Zeke could see the shadow again, clearly waving them on. "Let's go!"

The hikers hurried to where they had last seen the figure; again he disappeared.

"There!" said Willy, looking left.

There he was, moving up a small hill.

They reached the hill where the figure had been, and they looked around again. The sun was dropping below the horizon, and it was getting difficult to see.

"I can't see him."

"Neither can I."

Their eyes scanned their surroundings. Suddenly they saw a piece of black cloth tied to a branch about twenty feet away.

Zeke and Willy went over to investigate. The shred of black canvas was tied very carefully; one end stuck out at an angle.

Zeke moved around the bush and bent down. "Willy, get down here and look." Zeke pointed in the direction in which the strip of cloth pointed. "See anything?"

Willy squinted. "There's a branch straight ahead with another piece of cloth on it!"

They hurried to the other strip of cloth. It, too, was tied strangely; they peered in the direction that the longer end pointed.

"I don't see anything," said Willy.

"Walk in that direction," Zeke directed.

Willy made his way up the side of a small hill, stopped, then threw up his arms. "I don't see anything!"

"Wait for me!" Zeke called out. He reached the crest of the hill and looked around. The sun was now a faint orange glow on the western horizon.

Willy looked at his brother. "Do you suppose this shadow dude is the Samaritan stranger?"

Zeke shrugged.

"Maybe he's helping us figure out what to do."

Zeke slowly nodded in agreement. "OK, then, let's think." Zeke began pacing in the small area where they were standing. He looked up and thought out loud. "There's the sun. . . . That's west. . . . We've been going north on the trail, and a little east, mostly north. . . . The shelter was on the *left* side as we approached, so it's *west* of the trail. . . . And when you went to look for firewood . . . which way did you go?"

"I don't know," said Willy. "Into the woods."

"Away from the trail, right? You didn't cross the trail?"

"Right."

Zeke snapped his fingers. "And in all of our wandering, with the deer, with the stranger, all of that, we've *never* crossed the trail, right?"

"Right."

"*So,* whatever we have done, we have *not* traveled east. We have been west of the trail the whole time, which means we're west of the shelter, too! So if we travel that way, away from the setting sun, we will eventually reach the trail—and that will take us to the camp!"

"Bingo!"

Zeke and Willy scampered down the small elevation toward the east. Willy, who had the better eyesight, led the way.

"If we dropped our firewood, we could go faster," Willy suggested.

"Drop a piece or two," Zeke agreed, "but we may need some."

In about fifteen minutes, it was just about too dark to go anywhere. Willy scratched his face on a bush he didn't see. But they pushed on.

Suddenly Willy stopped. "Zeke, there aren't any trees here."

"Are you sure?"

Willy took some careful steps forward. "Yep. No trees."

"Well, if we're out of the woods, we can probably make a torch." Zeke quickly started building a small fire, grabbing some kindling from the underbrush and using the matches in his pocket.

From the light of the fire, Willy could see that they were on the trail. It extended upward to their right and downward to their left. Using a thin piece of their firewood, Zeke made a torch.

"Which way do we go?" Willy asked.

"Where was the shelter?" Zeke asked in return. "On a hill or in a valley?"

"It was just over a hill, near the top," Willy recalled.

Zeke was still thinking. "We've been over some small hills in our wandering, but nothing as big as the one near the shelter. And we've spent more time going down than going up. So I think we're pretty safe going up—don't you?"

Willy mumbled, "Um hmm."

They strode up the trial, with the torch lighting the way. Within ten minutes they saw the familiar walls of the

56

shelter. Chris and Pete were sitting on the ground; Sam was lying in his sleeping bag on his bunk.

Sam shot up. "Dudes!" he exclaimed. "We thought you guys were bear meat!"

"We were praying for you," Pete said. "We didn't know what else to do."

"Most excellent," said Zeke.

They lit a campfire that night from the torch that had led them back. Zeke told about the stranger who helped them, and Willy told of Zeke's brilliant logic.

No one ventured far from the others during the rest of the trip. And nothing matched the excitement of that evening.

When they returned to Millersburg, they thought no one would believe them about the stranger who helped them. But their story had the ring of truth.

THE END

Turn to page 141.

Town," Tina said finally, and Jill cheered.

"You girls always stick together," Jim complained, but he agreed to go with them. "Where do we start?"

"The Common," said Jill.

Jim moaned. "We've been there a million times!"

"You've been *through* it a million times, but have you ever really been *in* it?" Jill asked.

Jim looked puzzled. "What do you mean by that?"

"I don't know," Jill replied with a shrug. "It just sounded good."

So off they went to the Common, the park in the center of Millersburg. It was a wide expanse of green grass, turning brown in spots, with some huge trees here and there. People said that some of the trees dated back to the American Revolution. On the streets facing the Common were several shops, including the Freeze, plus the town hall and the old church whose bell the Ringers took their name from. The Whiteheads' grandfather was pastor of that church.

"First stop," said Jill, "the Great Oak." She and the Whitehead kids looked up at the towering tree.

"Planted in 1757 by Timothy Miller," Jim read from a plaque posted in front of the tree, "this was the meeting place of the Millersburg militia. It is said that George Washington gave a speech from this spot."

"Wow," said Tina. "George Washington."

"See what I mean?" said Jill. "You probably passed this tree lots of times without thinking of George Washington."

"I cannot tell a lie," Jim answered. "You're right. Now what else is in the Common?"

"Well," Jill said thoughtfully, biting the tip of her finger, "there's Ninepin Alley. Betty told me about it once. It's on the other side."

As the kids crossed the Common, they saw old Mr. Weatherly sitting on a park bench. He had white hair and was a bit hard of hearing. The cane he always used was propped against the bench. He greeted the three travelers cheerfully as they approached. They smiled and said hi.

"You're the one who's been helping Betty in the Freeze, aren't you?" he asked Jill.

"Yes, Mr. Weatherly. I'm Jill."

"Jill, could you do me a favor? I'm very thirsty out here, and I'm just too tired to walk back over there. Could you run over and get me a Coca-Cola? Betty knows me; she'll put it on my tab."

"Sure, Mr. Weatherly," said Jill. "I'd be happy to. Come on, guys. We'll be right back."

The three hikers changed course and headed for the Freeze. But as they were about to cross the street, they noticed a young woman in nice clothes walking down the sidewalk. She looked to be about twenty-five and had a shopping bag in her hand. Suddenly she stumbled for no apparent reason. She lurched forward for a few steps and then caught her balance again. She reached down and took a shoe from her foot, looked at the heel, then picked up the other piece of it, which had broken off the bottom of the shoe. She sat down on the sidewalk and started to cry.

"Should we help her out?" Jim asked. "It looks like she's in a fix."

"She probably just twisted her ankle," said Jill. "She'll be all right. Come on, we need to get Mr. Weatherly's Coke."

Jim hesitated. He remembered a story in the Bible about a man who got mugged while on a walk. Several people passed by without helping him, until finally a stranger stopped to help. Jim, Jill, and Tina had stopped to help Mr. Weatherly, but shouldn't they stop to help this woman first?

CHOICE ⇒

If Jim decides to stop and help the woman, turn to page 133.

If he decides to follow Jill's suggestion, turn to page 122.

Come on, Chris," said Willy. "It's not so bad. The rain won't make us shrink or anything. Let's keep going, like Zeke says."

It was Sam who seconded the motion. He didn't want to drag the rest of the guys down. Sure, he was hurting, but they had to move on.

Zeke led the way up the muddied path. The boys didn't talk much, even when Chris lost his footing and fell. He just got up and kept hiking, even though his pants were now covered with mud. The rain seemed to seep through their clothes and through their skin.

Fortunately, the air was warm—not hot, but comfortable—sort of like taking a shower . . . for four hours.

The rain stopped about half an hour before they reached the shelter. They each had a second set of clothing in their packs, and they looked forward to changing—if the rain had not gone through their backpacks.

As they approached the shelter, they saw three people milling around it. One was huddled over the concrete blocks that formed a fire pit. One was arranging his sleeping bag on one of the bunks in the shelter. A third person, who looked younger, was just sitting near the entrance of the shelter, looking out into the woods.

"Just what we need," muttered Chris, whose jeans were now thoroughly caked with mud and dirt. "Company."

"Yeah," said Willy. "Who invited them?"

Zeke stopped suddenly and turned to face them. "That's no way to think," he said, glaring especially at his younger brother. "I mean, who invited *us?* We're all guests here, and we need to treat our fellow travelers with kindness and respect."

"But is there going to be room for us?" Chris asked.

"That's a rule of the trail," Zeke explained. "There's always room. Now let's go meet them."

Zeke's little band descended on the clearing. The three other travelers looked up.

"Greetings!" said the man at the fire.

"How are you?" said Zeke, stepping forward to shake the man's hand. "I'm Clarence Washington. My friends call me Zeke."

"I'm Bob Presser," said the man, with a warm press from Zeke's hand. "That's my brother, Bill, and my son, Robby."

Bill waved from the shelter. Robby kept looking into the woods.

"Well, this is my crew," Zeke said. "My brother, Willy. Chris, Pete, and Sam." The boys nodded in greeting.

"I see you got caught in the rain," Bob said in a big voice that seemed much too friendly. "If I ever get a fire going, you can dry out a bit."

"We can probably start our own fire," said Chris. He felt uneasy sharing the space with strangers.

Bob went on as if Chris hadn't said anything. "We got

here just as the rain started, so we were fortunate. We've been killing time all afternoon waiting for it to stop. It's a beautiful thing to look at, but not so fun when you're hiking in it."

"Tell me about it!" Zeke laughed.

"So you'll be moving on now?" Chris suggested.

"No, it's almost sundown. I'm sure they'll stay here tonight." It was Zeke who answered.

"Yeah," said Bob. "We'll just scrunch up in one corner of the shelter and let you have the rest. They usually make these things to hold eight or ten, so we shouldn't have any problem."

Bill Presser, the brother, joined the conversation. "So," Bill said, "are you going to join us for dinner and the campfire?"

"I think it's a great idea," said Zeke, but he noticed Chris and Willy stiffen a bit at the thought. "But maybe I'd better check it out with the guys here. They may have had some plans for tonight."

Zeke rounded up the four boys and took them to another part of the clearing, where they talked softly.

"So what do you want to do?" Zeke asked.

Chris spoke first. "We don't know who they are. I just don't feel like listening to a bunch of strangers talk."

"Yeah," said Willy, "I feel the same way. I mean, this is our trip, and they're having their trip. Let's just keep them separate."

"You guys are unbelievable," said Zeke. "Here we are out in nature, enjoying what God has created. And part of that nature is *people*. God created them too. I think it's kind of fun to get to know other people along the way. Believe me, we're going to get to know each other real well. Here's a chance to reach out a little.

"But I'll let you guys call it. You can be geeks if you want to. What'll it be?"

If they decide to join the other hikers for dinner and the campfire, turn to page 128.

If they decide to stay separate from the others, turn to page 115.

Scared out of his wits, Chris could only answer back:
"GRRRRRRRRRRRRRRRRRRRRRRRRRRRRRRR!"

There was a furious rustle in the bushes, and the dark
shape emerged. Chris heard a horrible voice saying, "I'M
GOING TO EAT YOU UP!"

"NO!" Chris shouted, covering his face. He cringed in
the terrible silence, waiting for the death blow.

Wait a minute. . . .

He pulled his hands down from his eyes and saw his
best friend, Willy, standing two feet away with a wide grin
on his face.

"Gotcha!"

Without a word, Chris turned and walked toward
camp. Willy followed him, with that smile still parked on his
face. For about a minute, neither said a word. But Willy
couldn't hold it in any longer.

"OH NO, MISTER BEAR!" he squealed. "DON'T EAT
ME!"

Chris was not in a good mood. His feet itched, his
jeans were wet, his heart was pounding, and now he would
never be able to show his face in public again. He was not
a happy camper.

But Willy was bouncing all around him, mimicking
him, teasing him, growling. "Chris, you were hysterical! I
wish I had a video camera with me!"

"Why didn't you?" Chris snapped. "You thought of everything else." Chris turned and faced his pal. "You set me up! All of that stuff about the bears—"

"I made it up."

For the first time, Chris smiled, shaking his head. "Don't tell anybody, all right?"

"What's it worth to you?"

Chris thought for a moment. "Your life," he said calmly. "Come on, we'd better get back before it's dark."

"Yeah," Willy agreed. "In another hour or so the tigers come out."

Chris gave his friend a shove that sent Willy sprawling forward. Regaining his feet, Willy put up his hands. "All right, I deserved it. But I've got an idea. You want to hear it?"

"I've had enough of your ideas, Willy. We need to hurry back."

"It's not far now, and this'll be great, Chris. We can sneak up on Sam and Pete and scare them just like I scared you."

"What about Zeke?"

"My brother's probably tending the fire. I bet Sam and Pete are in their tent. That'll be perfect."

"I don't know." Chris just wanted to get back to camp so he could take his stupid boots off.

But scaring the others could be fun.

Still, it was getting dark, and—bears or no bears—Chris was afraid they might get lost.

But he liked the idea of scaring someone else. That way he wouldn't be the only one Willy would make fun of.

So many choices. . . .

66

CHOICE

If Chris and Willy scare the others, turn to page 17.
If they head straight to camp, turn to page 102.

The light shined brightly in Sam's eyes. He squinted and blinked.

He sat up quickly and looked around, rubbing his eyes. He was in his sleeping bag in the bunk of the shelter. It took a moment for him to realize that it was morning. Where was Pete?

"I don't know what you were dreaming about this time," said Pete from across the clearing, "but it sure must have been exciting. You were tossing and turning like a Mexican jumping bean. Wrestling that wolf again?"

Suddenly a sense of relief came over Sam. "No, just finding terrorists in the woods."

Pete yawned. "Is that all?"

"Isn't it enough? I hang around with you too much. *That's* the problem."

"You don't hang around him *enough*," Willy's brother broke in. Zeke was cooking breakfast—freeze-dried eggs and bacon. Sam went over and took a whiff.

To Sam's surprise, it smelled good. "Ah, the smooth aroma of a fake breakfast on a fine summer day." He smiled widely.

"So you were dreaming about terrorists, eh?"

"Yeah, man. Cuban ones." Sam felt a chill and shuddered aloud.

Zeke noticed but did not look up as the guys gathered around. "It seemed real, didn't it?"

"I've got a wound right here," Sam joked, pointing to his stomach. Everyone laughed and then fell silent, watching Zeke cook.

"Sometimes when I'm having a nightmare," Pete said, "I realize I'm dreaming and I want to wake up, but I can't. So I keep telling myself, 'It's just a dream. It's just a dream.' It's like I can make it through the nightmare because I believe in awakeness."

Everyone nodded in agreement.

Zeke chuckled. "The morning always comes, too, don't it brothers?"

"Amen to that," Willy mumbled.

Zeke rearranged the sort of eggs and sort of bacon that were sort of sizzling in the pan. "Someday we'll all wake up." He smiled at his four young charges. "Always believe in the morning, gentlemen, for one day this nightmare will be over!"

Just then Sam leaned over, pointed at the pan, and asked, *"This* nightmare?"

Zeke glared at him. *"Life,"* he said simply.

"Sam's just looking forward to eating heavenly hash," said Willy with a chuckle.

A little more rearranging and Zeke suddenly announced, "Breakfast is served!" The guys scrambled to pull tiny plates and forks out of their packs, and Zeke served a humble portion to each. As it turned out, the meal smelled better than it tasted. Zeke's hopes that they wouldn't complain about the food were dashed as the guys competed to see who could make the look of greatest disgust. But these hikers were hungry, and they ate every bite anyway.

"The food in heaven will be much better, gentlemen," he assured them. "If you can't stand my cooking, just believe in the morning. You'll make it through."

"We'll try, Brother," Willy consoled him with a pat on the back.

"Hey, who's doing the dishes?" asked Sam.

"*You* are," Zeke said matter-of-factly.

"Is that another part of this nightmare that'll come to an end in heaven?" Chris asked.

"Uh huh."

"Let us cheerfully do the dishes, Kimosabes!" Sam announced in a dramatic voice, "knowing that one day, all . . . dishes . . . will . . . clean . . . THEMSELVES!"

"YEA!" they all cheered.

And with that, the crew started another day.

THE END

Was it only a dream? Or was it real? If you still aren't sure, turn to page 28 and make different choices along the way.

Or, turn to page 141.

Come on, Jill!" Tina pleaded. "Don't be a spoilsport. It'll be fun!"

But Jill had been imagining all the great adventures the boys would have on their hike. She had been jealous of their fun. But she knew that if she tried to take a "hike" around Millersburg, it wouldn't be nearly as much fun.

"Come on, Jill!" It was Jim this time. "Forget about the other guys."

No, Jill thought. A hike around town would just remind her of the fun she was *not* having. She just didn't want to go.

"I've got an idea," said Tina. "It's probably dumb."

"No," Jim answered, "tell us."

"Let's go to the library, get a map, and find out where they went."

"Great idea!" said Jim. "Let's go!"

It didn't take much to convince Jill to come along.

The Blue Ridge hikers were having a great time. They all seemed to be enjoying each other.

"Look at that!" Zeke said, and the boys stopped behind him. There was a chipmunk picking up a nut from the ground as a bird looked on. Both seemed frozen, staring each other down.

"I bet the bird gets the nut," Chris whispered.

"I don't bet," said Pete, "but the chipmunk will keep it."

Willy kept staring at the creatures and softly said, "I bet a bear comes and eats them both."

Chris snorted with laughter, which distracted the chipmunk, who dropped the nut, which was snatched up by the bird, who flew up to a branch, which snapped, causing the bird to shriek, dropping the nut, which fell on the chipmunk's back, scaring the chipmunk, who scurried a few feet away, then turned and saw the nut. But by now the bird had flown back down and was also a few feet from the nut. The two creatures stared each other down again.

"This could take all day," Chris joked, and the hikers moved on.

Jill, Tina, and Jim sauntered over to a huge book on a slanted desk top. It was an atlas. They opened it up and flipped pages until they came to a map of the Blue Ridge Mountains of Virginia. They soon located a thin, winding ribbon marked Appalachian Trail.

"Here's where the boys went," Jill told her friends. She traced her finger along the trail.

It was getting late. Willy's feet felt heavy. Zeke said they were close to the shelter where they would stay the night. He said it was just over the next hill, but that was like saying it was on Mars. Willy wasn't sure how much farther he could go. The other boys felt pretty much the same. This hiking stuff was hard work. It had been a fun day, full of great sights and good friendship, but they all looked forward to putting their feet up.

"Come on, guys," Zeke called from about ten feet in front of them. "You can do it. We're almost there."

"That's what you said half an hour ago," cracked Willy.

"Well," said Zeke, "we're a half hour closer then, aren't we?"

As they crested the hill, they looked down into a small clearing. There was the shelter, at last. Of course it wasn't the Holiday Inn, but for hikers it was close enough.

The shelter had just three walls and a slanted roof. Inside, all along the walls, were wide shelves that hikers used as bunk beds. In the middle of the clearing, a few cement blocks were arranged as a sort of fireplace. This spot held the ashes of many a campfire.

The boys quickly claimed their bunks, dropping their backpacks. Willy sat and began to untie his shoes.

"Not so fast, Bro," said Zeke, standing above him. "It's your turn to get firewood."

Willy looked up pleadingly. "Now?"

Zeke nodded. "The sooner we have wood, the sooner we eat."

Willy sighed heavily and trooped back into the woods for some wood.

It wasn't always easy to find good firewood. You couldn't just pull branches from trees. That would hurt the trees, and the branches would be too green to burn very well anyhow. You needed branches that had fallen naturally and quite some time ago, so they'd be dry. Willy roamed among the trees, scanning the ground for twigs and logs.

After gathering a few small branches, he sat down and looked around him. There, only twenty feet in front of him, was a deer. It had its head down—searching for food, Willy figured—but then it looked up, saw Willy, and froze. For a moment, they held each other's stare—the tired boy and the beautiful deer.

Willy imagined that they were talking to each other.

"Why are you here in my woods?"

"I'm just passing through, my friend. I mean you no harm."

"Good. Then we can share it."

"It is a beautiful place."

"I like it."

The deer broke the gaze and bounded off to Willy's left. Something in Willy wanted to follow the deer.

CHOICE

If Willy follows the deer, turn to page 91.

If Willy returns to camp, turn to page 137.

What is this?" Willy asked defensively. "The Spanish Inquisition? I can find my way back."

With that, the stranger turned on his heel and strode away quickly. Willy watched him take a few steps, and then the man seemed to vanish.

Strange, Willy thought. Then he resumed his pacing. Five hundred paces, turn, five hundred paces, turn. Soon he realized he was going in circles—well, squares. So he decided to turn a different direction, but then he forgot which direction to turn, so he was even more lost than before.

And the sun was setting.

Maybe I wandered farther than I thought, he thought. *Why aren't they calling for me?*

When he finally decided to cry out for help, he was too tired to shout much. His weak voice did not carry far. As darkness fell, he leaned against a tree and considered his options. *Well, I could walk around a lot and then sit down here, or I could just sit down here. I think I'll sit down here.*

And in the deep darkness he fell asleep. He dreamed that he was the Appalachian Samaritan Zeke had told him about—wandering the mountains, offering help to those in need. People would respect him for his knowledge of the wilderness. People would look up to him. People would marvel at him. "Willy!" they would call out. "Willy of the

Appalachians, come and help us!" And he would stride in and give them the food they needed, or bind up their wounds, or show them the way. "Thank you, Willy!" they would say. "Willy, you are so cool! Hooray for Willy! Willy!"

"Willy!" the voices were saying. "Where have you been?" He opened his eyes to see three blurry figures approach him.

"Willy! Thank God we found you!"

"Willy! You're so cold. Here, take my jacket."

It was morning. His friends had come to look for him. It was Chris and Pete and Zeke, bending over to him, helping him up. Sam had stayed at the shelter to guard their equipment.

"Are you all right?"

"You sure had us scared."

"I'm so glad that man told us where to find you."

"Come on back to the shelter, Willy. You need a few hours in a warm sleeping bag."

They led Willy back to camp.

The hikers took it easy that day, which was good for Chris, whose feet were killing him, and Willy, who felt stiff all over.

They broke camp the next day and moved along the trail.

THE END

If you haven't found out what happens to Sam's shoulder, turn to page 28 and make different choices along the way.

Or, turn to page 141.

Bethel Baptist Church
Sykesville, Pa.

"Tell you what," Tina said to the runaway, "we'll give you the blanket if you tell us why you ran away."

"Give me the blanket first!" the boy cried. He still seemed to be afraid of them.

"No," said Tina. "You tell us first, and then we'll give you the blanket."

"I don't believe you!" the boy said.

Tina took hold of the blanket and asked Jim and Jill to step back. "You can believe me, Kenny," she said in a caring voice. "I just want to help you. You have to talk to me. How long have you been out here?"

"A couple of days," Kenny answered.

"Do you like it out here?"

"It's OK," Kenny said, his foot pawing the ground. "Better than home."

"What's wrong with home?" Tina asked.

"Rules. Too many rules."

"Yeah," Tina said, nodding, "that can be rough." She let go of the blanket and stepped back. "Here's your blanket."

The boy greedily grabbed the opposite corner of the blanket and pulled it to him.

"Hey, Kenny," Tina called, "we're going up to the water tower. You can come if you want. It's up to you." With that, she turned and walked away. Jim and Jill went along. Kenny watched them for a long time and then started to follow them.

The three Ringers broke out of the woods, into an open space, and looked upward. There was a water tower, the height of a five-story building. It was painted white with green letters at the top that simply spelled "Historic Millersburg." It had not been used for a long while, and its legs and rungs were spotted with peeling paint and rust. A chain link fence surrounded it, but that had fallen down in some places and was cut through in others.

Jim ducked through a hole in the fence. "Well, I'm climbing it," he said. "Anyone want to join me?"

Now that they saw it, neither Jill nor Tina cared to climb it. It was awfully tall, and they didn't trust those rungs.

"Come on!" Jim repeated. "Won't anyone come up with me?"

A squeaky voice came from the edge of the woods. "I will."

Bravely Kenny walked forward and gave his blanket to Tina. Then he ducked through the fence to join Jim.

"Hi, Kenny. My name's Jim. Just follow me."

But Kenny was already in front of Jim, running to the east side of the tower and up the rungs of the tower's ladder. Jim playfully gave chase. The steps were rusted here and there, but Jim watched for those spots and avoided them. Kenny was light and darted up the steps easily. Jim was larger and had to be more careful. In a few minutes they reached the rusty catwalk that circled the middle of the water tank. They carefully walked around to the west side of the tower.

It was true. You could see Millersburg from there. Not all of it, but the eastern side of the town was in full view. Jim could just see one side of the Common, and over the trees he saw the steeple tower of the Capitol Community Church. That's where the Ringers' bell was.

Kenny was amazed to see so much in one glance—Millersburg, the woods, and Forest Creek.

"Is that where you live?" Jim asked. "Forest Creek?"

"Used to," said Kenny. "I live in the woods now."

"Oh yeah." Jim nodded. "I forgot." There was silence for a minute as they both enjoyed the view. Then Jim spoke up again. "What rules didn't you like?"

"Mom's rules. Dad's rules. Mom's rules. Dad's rules. Drives you crazy. Can't do Mom's rules when you're at Dad's. Can't do Dad's when you're at Mom's."

Jim didn't know what to say. "They just have rules because they love you," he tried. It was the wrong thing to say.

"No," Kenny said strongly. "No. No. They don't even know I'm gone."

"Of course they do," Jim replied. "They're probably looking for you right now."

"No. No. No," Kenny shook his head frantically from side to side. "Dad thinks I'm with Mom. Mom thinks I'm with Dad. None of them wants me."

"Don't talk like that."

"I can talk however I want. I'm a little boy in a little house in a little town in a little world—and I can't take it anymore."

Jim stretched his hand toward the horizon. "Look at that, Kenny. Look at all that stuff. The woods. Your town, my town. The church steeple. I know who made all of that. It's God. He made me and he made you. And I know he loves me. He loves you too, Kenny. And he's big. Real big."

"NO!" Kenny said violently. He went tramping back to the steps. "No! No! No! No! No!" Suddenly a rusty part of the catwalk near the steps broke beneath his feet. He fell through the catwalk but managed to grab onto the bottom pole of railing that ran around the catwalk. Jim was a step behind and reached for him as he broke through, but missed. Kenny was hanging from the catwalk, four and half stories from the ground. Jim grabbed his wrist and tried to pull him back up, but couldn't.

"I have to go for help, Kenny. I'll be right back," Jim said.

"NO!" Kenny screamed. "Don't leave me!" His eyes were wild with panic.

Jim realized that this whole section of catwalk was in danger of collapsing. Whenever he moved, he felt it give more. Kenny had a grip on the railing, and Jim couldn't pull him back. It seemed more dangerous for them both if Jim stayed there. But in Kenny's present state of mind, he might give up and let go before help arrived. Jim wasn't sure what to do.

CHOICE ⇒

If Jim goes to get help, turn to page 106.

If Jim stays with Kenny, turn to page 14.

Zeke insisted that he could find the way back to camp. He tried retracing their steps, but they had taken so many—as Willy chased the deer and Zeke followed Willy—that it was hopeless.

The sun was going down and the woods were growing dark, but still Zeke refused to call out for help. It would be embarrassing for the most experienced hiker to get lost. Zeke was determined to find the way.

But he couldn't.

When night fell, Zeke finally gave up. They would have to sleep in the woods.

Willy was amazed at how dark it was. With no city lights anywhere nearby, and the tiny amount of moonlight blocked out by the trees overhead, the darkness was nearly total. He could hardly see his hand in front of his face. The brothers did their best to create a bed for themselves from the leaves on the floor of the woods, but it was very uncomfortable.

They tried to make the best of things by talking about growing up, reliving stories of their childhood. It helped, but it didn't keep the bugs away.

When the next day dawned, Zeke and Willy were quite tired. It had taken a long time for each of them to get to sleep, and they had awakened with bug bites all over. Willy had a stiff neck and Zeke was sneezing.

It was still fairly early when they heard voices. Chris and Pete were out looking for them as Sam held down the fort at the shelter. The reunion was a happy one, considering how miserable the Washington boys were.

"We were incredibly worried about you!" said Pete, as he ran toward them. "Did you guys get lost?"

"Yes!" Zeke growled.

"But I thought you knew—," Chris started to say, but was cut short by a mighty sneeze from Zeke.

"Bless you," said the three other hikers to their embarrassed guide.

"Thanks," sniffed Zeke. "Why don't you guys lead us back to camp." And as he trudged back to the shelter, Zeke thought about the lesson he had learned: Even an experienced hiker has to admit when he needs help.

THE END

To find out what other exciting adventures the Ringers have along the trail, turn to page 70 and make different choices along the way.

Or, turn to page 141.

82

It was well past midnight when Sam awoke. "Pete," he whispered. "You awake?"

"Now I am," Pete answered. "What's up?"

"I have to go."

"Bye."

"No," Sam said more urgently. "I have to go to the bathroom."

"End of the hall on the right," Pete growled.

"No! I have to go out *there*."

Pete rolled over in his sleeping bag. "Right. Have fun."

"Can you come with me?"

Pete opened his eyes. *"What?"*

"Can . . . you . . . come . . . with . . . me," Sam said distinctly.

"Why?"

"Because it's dark out there. And there might be, like, porcupines."

"I thought you didn't believe in porcupines."

"Come on, Pete. I have to go!"

"All right." Pete reluctantly climbed out of his bunk. "I'll defend you from wild porcupines while you do your business."

They ventured out about thirty yards from the shelter.

As they were returning, Sam stopped.

"What is it now, Sam?" Pete whispered, impatiently.

"Do you hear that?"

"What?"

"Voices."

Pete heard them too. Three men's voices, sounding surprisingly close.

"We won't get caught," said one voice. "We'll do it right. We won't get caught."

"You take out your people, and I'll take out mine," said a second voice. "It's that simple."

"But how do we infiltrate their inner circle?" It was the first voice again. "We have to get someone on the inside."

"Juan's got it covered," said a third voice, deeper than the others.

"He has a contact?" the second voice asked.

"He *is* the contact," the deeper voice responded.

There was silence for a few moments. Then the first man asked, "What's our code word?"

"Summertime."

Someone laughed. "And the livin' is easy."

"You bet."

Sam was clutching Pete's arm. "There's something very wrong happening out here," he said softly. "Verrrrrry wrong."

CHOICE ⟹

If Sam and Pete investigate the situation, turn to page 98.

84

If they go back to the shelter and tell Zeke about this, turn to page 23.

If they decide to ignore it, turn to page 7.

Chris kept quiet about his role in the prank. Willy had to bear the brunt of Zeke's fury all by himself. After his older brother called him "immature" and "irresponsible," Willy shouted back, "I was only trying to have some fun!" Then he walked away.

"That's it!" Zeke said, suddenly standing up. "We're going home. Sorry, guys, but you'd better pack up. We're out of here."

They talked him into staying the night, since it was too dark to travel, but in the morning Zeke and Willy still weren't talking. Zeke led them back the way they had come, and the boys rode back to Millersburg in Zeke's car without saying a word.

The Appalachian Adventure was over.

THE END

If you haven't found out what Willy chases through the forest, turn to page 64 and make different choices along the way.

Or, turn to page 141.

All right," said Zeke, looking slowly around at all the hikers. "Let's stop for a short break. Look, there's a place we can sit down." He pointed to a place to their left, where a tree had fallen.

They scrambled through some underbrush to the tree and sat down. Zeke stood in front of Sam and put his hands on Sam's shoulders.

"Which one is it, Sam?"

"The right."

"Does that hurt?"

"Yes. Owww!"

"Sorry. Can you do this?" Zeke raised his arm in the air. Sam raised his partway and cried out in pain. The other boys looked over at him.

"Are you all right?" Pete asked.

"Perfect health," Sam replied through a moan, "as long as I don't move or breathe. Otherwise, I'm three-quarters dead."

"Well," said Zeke, putting his hand to his chin, "I'm not a doctor—"

"But he plays one on TV!" Willy teased.

"Come on, Will," Zeke said with a sigh. "I think Sam pulled a muscle. The good news is that you'll be fine—eventually. The bad news is that it will hurt like crazy for a couple of days."

"Carrying a backpack requires breathing," said Sam, lying back along the length of the tree trunk. "I don't think I can carry a backpack any farther."

"I know," said Zeke as he walked away.

From his pack, Chris took out a small container of gorp, a trail mix of raisins and nuts, and offered some to Sam after taking a handful himself. Pete sat on the ground, his back against another tree, and prayed silently for his friend. Zeke stood a few steps off and studied the map of the trail.

After a few minutes, Zeke addressed his troops. "Men, I think I figured something out. In a couple of miles, we'll be crossing a road that crosses the mountains. And that's just a couple of miles from a small town, where we can get a bus back to the lodge where we parked the car."

"You mean . . . go home?" Chris asked.

"Yes," said Zeke. "We'd be going home. It's a bad break, but there's not much else we can do. Sam can't carry a pack for the next day or two."

"We can carry it for him," Chris protested.

"I know, but it'll get really heavy really fast," Zeke answered. "It's no fun lugging extra gear around. And I think Sam just wants to go home and rest."

"Just leave me here, guys," said Sam dramatically. "Don't stop for my sake. Save yourselves!"

"Yeah," Chris agreed. "Sam's a tough guy. He can take it. We don't need to go home. What do you say, Willy? Pete?"

Willy and Pete weren't sure. Willy kind of agreed with Chris. It wasn't as if Sam was dying or anything. Pete thought that going home might be a better idea. They'd have other chances to hike. But then he worried that Sam would feel guilty for spoiling everyone else's fun. He didn't know which would hurt most, the pain or the guilt. So he wasn't sure what to do.

"So Willy and I want to keep hiking," Chris summed up, "and Sam doesn't want to ruin things and Pete's not sure. So I think that means we should keep hiking."

Zeke turned his back suddenly, paced a few times, and then turned to face them. The boys could see he was angry. "Who's leading this group, Chris? You or me?"

"Well, you are, Zeke, but I thought it was, like, a democracy."

"And why am I leading this group?"

"Because you've done it a lot. You know a lot about hiking."

"That's right, Chris." Zeke seemed to be searching the sky for the words to say. "I know what it's like to hike with a bad back, and I know what it's like to carry someone else's pack. I also know that the best thing sometimes is to say, 'Hey, we tried—let's try again later.' Now this map tells me we have a chance to cut the trip short. It's an hour to the road, another hour to the town. If we make the bus, we could get to the lodge by seven and be home by midnight. If we don't do this now, it'll be a day and a half before we have that option again. I have figured this out, Chris, and I don't like it either. But I'm responsible for the well-being of all you guys, including Sam, and this is what I recommend—for Sam's sake."

CHOICE ⟹

If they decide to cut the trip short, turn to page 9.

If they decide to keep hiking, turn to page 24.

Zeke did not like being awakened in the middle of the night. He did not like hearing crazy stories about spies and terrorists. If this was some sort of prank, he was not amused. He just wanted to go back to sleep.

Which he did.

Sam panicked. He had a feeling—he just had a feeling that Zeke was wrong. Still, what could he do?

That's when Sam made a decision. He was not going to let Zeke take this lying down.

"Clarence Washington," Sam whispered loudly in Zeke's face, "wake up right now. This is not a drill. If this had been a fake emergency, you would have heard a beep and then a calm male voice announcing that this was just an emergency. But this is NOT a test of the Emergency Broadcast System. THIS IS A REAL EMERGENCY, SO WILL YOU PLEASE WAKE UP RIGHT NOW?"

Zeke opened his eyes. Whether he liked it or not, he was awake. "OK," he said in a conciliatory tone. "I'm up."

Turn to page 118.

Willy chased after the swift deer. He saw a flash of brown in front of him and followed. Just when he thought he lost the trail, the deer would seem to stop and wait. But when Willy got close, the animal would bound off in another direction. Or maybe that was just Willy's imagination.

It was great fun. He forgot all about his tired feet. He was out in the wild, playing hide-and-seek with a deer. *Just wait till the guys hear about this,* Willy thought.

WHOMP!

Willy tripped over a fallen branch and landed flat on his face. His nose was now planted in the leafy undergrowth of the woods. The leaves actually cushioned his fall; otherwise, he might have broken something.

He looked up for the deer. He half expected it to come running back with a look that said, "Are you all right?" But he saw nothing.

Getting back to his feet, Willy looked at the thick branch that caused his fall. *Hmmm,* he thought, *that would be great for firewood.*

Then he remembered why he was out there. The other guys were probably waiting impatiently, wondering where he was. They'd be hungry and growing cold, and they'd give him a hard time. *Better get back,* Willy thought, picking up the branch. *But where is "back"?*

He had completely lost all sense of direction. The chase had turned him around so completely that he had no idea where the shelter was.

Why not just call out for help? he asked himself. *I couldn't have gone very far. They're probably still within earshot.*

But then they'll tease me for the rest of the trip. "Witless Willy can't even gather firewood without getting lost! Better put a leash on him." That would be embarrassing. Maybe if I just go this way, I can find my way back.

Willy walked for fifty paces or so, but nothing looked familiar, so he turned right and walked another fifty paces. He thought again about calling out. *But maybe that would be dumb. I'm probably really close.*

If Willy calls out for help, turn to page 32.

If he tries to find his own way, turn to page 5.

The woods seem more exciting," Tina said finally. "Let's go there."

So they set out for the woods. It began a few blocks behind the memorial and stretched about a half mile south to where the Forest Creek development began. On the east side was the old water tower, which hadn't been used for twenty years.

Jim had seen the tower from the road whenever he rode with his grandfather into Washington, but he had never seen it up close. It had always seemed interesting to him, like some sort of round flying saucer perched on a tall tripod. "I suppose if you climb the tower you can see the whole town," said Jim as they made their way through the trees.

"Well, if you wanted to see the town," joked Jill, "we could have stayed there." She was happy to have friends around to do stuff with. It had felt so lonely when the other boys left on their trip, and she was glad to be making some excitement of her own.

The three wound their way eastward, through the trees, admiring the greenery and the occasional animals they saw. They were getting close to the water tower when they saw a blanket on the ground. There was an empty tin can nearby, and some ashes from a fire.

"Looks like someone else has been here," said Jill.

Suddenly Tina saw something dart through the woods. "What's that?" she gasped. The others looked in the direction she pointed, but saw nothing. They began to move on, but there was a rustle of leaves, and Jill saw a movement out of the corner of her eye. "There's something there," she said.

Jim put his finger to his lips, indicating quiet. "Let's go," he whispered. They took two steps, then Jim turned around suddenly—just in time to see a boy run from one tree to another, a little bit behind them. "There he is!" Jim yelled and ran toward the boy. The boy turned and ran into the woods.

"Who was that?" Tina asked.

Jill shrugged. "He looked dirty."

"Do you think he's the one camping out here?" asked Tina.

"I bet he is," said Jim, returning from his brief chase. "I think I know how we can find out." Jim picked up the blanket by a corner. The bottom was covered with dirt and leaves. In a loud voice, Jim said, "Oh, what a nice blanket! I guess it doesn't belong to anybody. Let's take it along with us." And he began to walk away with it.

Suddenly a squeaky voice came from behind them. "That's my blanket!"

The three Ringers turned.

The boy was standing between two trees. He looked about eight years old, with dirty blond hair that was, as a matter of fact, quite dirty. His T-shirt and jeans also had streaks of dirt on them.

"Sorry," Jim said. "But how do we know it's yours?"

"'Cause it is," the boy said.

"Are you living out here?" asked Tina.

The boy looked down at the ground. "Sort of."

"The ground is probably cold and wet at night, isn't it?" Tina said. The boy nodded. "What's your name?" she asked.

"Kenny."

"You ran away from home," Jim guessed, "didn't you?"

The boy was suddenly afraid. "Give me my blanket!" he demanded.

"Look, guys," said Jill, "I think we're bothering him. Why don't we just give him the blanket and move on?"

Tina's eyes were full of pity for this boy. "Maybe we can help him," she suggested.

CHOICE ⇒

If they try to help the boy, turn to page 76.

If they leave him alone, turn to page 21.

No way," said Chris. "I'm not saying I'm sorry when I didn't do anything wrong. If Zeke doesn't like it, that's his problem. I'm tired of him bossing us around."

"Fine," Zeke answered. "If you're going to be that way about it, fine. I was just trying to do what was best."

"What *you thought* was best," Chris shot back.

"I thought you were more mature than this, Chris."

"What does that mean?"

The conversation only got uglier. The group did continue their journey—for a day. But there were such bad feelings between Chris and Zeke that they decided to cut the trip short after all—which was fine with Sam, even though he insisted that they leave him in a ditch.

Willy did some major diplomacy at home during the next few days, going back and forth between Zeke and Chris, trying to patch things up. Eventually, apologies were exchanged, and both were pretty embarrassed about the whole thing.

In addition, the hikers had to hear the great tales of Jill, Tina, and Jim—in their exploits in and around Millersburg. The guys who had been in the mountains had to admit that they had a whole different kind of adventure.

THE END

To find out what other crazy hiking adventures the Ringers have, turn to page 28 and make different choices along the way.

Or, turn to page 141.

Let's find out what it is," Pete whispered back.

"Don't you think we should tell Zeke?" Sam cautioned.

"Eventually," Pete replied. "But we don't even know what's going on yet. Come on!"

Pete crept toward the sound. Reluctantly, Sam followed. They were as quiet as they could be, but each time they heard voices, they edged forward a bit more.

The voices continued.

"Let's review the plan."

"Again?"

"It has to go like clockwork."

"All right."

"Monday's a holiday, so there's a skeleton staff. Juan will disarm the security systems and open the vault doors so we can get in without setting off the alarms."

"Do we have the trucks?"

"They are being *procured* as we speak. They'll be stenciled to look like the real thing."

"So our phony guards take the next shift after we bag the real guards. And we drive in and take what we want. They won't know what hit them until we're back in Cuba."

"And we, gentlemen, will have all the gold."

"The American dogs will have to honor the Revolution then."

"Who would have thought that we could rob Fort Knox?"

Sam and Pete had moved very close to the voices now. They were seeing vague shapes in the darkness, people seated on logs, on the ground. There was no fire, no light. Only three or four shapes, and Sam and Pete perched at the edge of their circle.

"Hey, José, you got a cigarette?"

"I thought you quit."

"I'm trying. But this makes me nervous."

"Here."

Sam realized what was coming and backed away. Pete did not. Cigarette means smoke. Smoke means fire. Fire means light.

The man struck a match that briefly lit up the scene—four men seated, and Pete standing not three feet away. Sam was already several steps away.

"What's that?"

Pete was a sitting duck.

"Light another match."

Pete tried to scamper away, but a hand shot out to grab his arm.

"What do we have here? A spy? An American spy sent to thwart the Revolution?"

Sam was twenty feet away, trying to see what was going on. Pete was thrown into the middle of the circle. Somebody grabbed a flashlight and shined it in Pete's face.

"Who are you?"

"Who are you working for?"

Pete gulped loudly. "I'm just a kid! Honest! We're on a—I mean, I'm on a hiking trip."

"How old are you?" the deep voice growled.

"Fourteen. I'll be fifteen in September."

One voice let out a laugh. "I see the CIA is growing them younger."

The deep voice ignored the comment and began to interrogate Pete. "So you're on a hiking trip? Where are the others?"

Pete wanted to protect the other hikers. The shelter was not far away, and he knew Sam was out there somewhere. "What others?"

"Do you think we are stupid? A fourteen-year-old boy does not hike in the woods at night by himself."

"No," Pete said nervously. "They're a long way up the trail. A long way. I got lost. I'm trying to find them."

"They did not wait for you?"

"No," Pete said, thinking quickly. "They don't like me very much."

"What do you think, gentlemen," the deep voice queried. "Maybe he is just a kid."

"Here's a wallet, señor." Someone ripped Pete's thin billfold from his back pocket.

The flashlight was trained on the wallet as a pair of stubby, stained hands flipped through its contents. "A junior high I.D. A few dollars. A baseball card."

"Football," Pete corrected. "Deacon Joe Johnson of the Redskins."

"I see," the voice went on. "What's this? An electronic box of some sort."

"Oh," Pete stammered. "Th-that's just a n-new layout for the case of a computer I'm m-making."

"What kind of fourteen-year-old makes computers?"

"I do, sir. It's a hobby. I'm kind of smart."

"You're kind of smart, but you get lost in the woods. That does not compute." The man laughed suddenly at his own joke.

"Believe me!" Pete pleaded.

"And what have we here?" The stubby fingers pulled another card from the wallet, a pass to get into FBI headquarters. "You were very wrong, Manuel, when you suggested our friend was from the CIA. He seems to be from the FBI."

Pete was floored. "That's just for my father. He works at the FBI building, that's all. That pass is so I can visit him at work."

"And he sent you here to spy on us."

"No!"

The man trained the flashlight back on Pete's face, but as he moved it, the beam of light crossed Sam, who was listening from a distance.

"Wait," someone said. "Shine the flashlight over there."

Sam panicked. He could run away, but that would mean leaving Pete—and he might lead these guys to the other hikers, and then they'd all be in trouble. But if he didn't run—what then?

CHOICE ⇒

If Sam runs away, turn to page 40.

If Sam doesn't, turn to page 127.

My feet are killing me, Willy," said Chris. "I just want to go back to camp and take off these shoes. All right?"

With that, Chris started walking faster.

"Chris!" Willy yelped before taking off after his friend.

"Look," Chris continued, "if you want to scare them, fine. I'll even pretend to be scared with them."

"No, it's not the same."

"Sure it is, Willy. You can growl and rustle the bushes, and it'll be hysterical."

"No," Willy repeated. "It won't work."

"I don't see why not. Sam and Pete know as little as I do about camping out. They'll fall for it. And as long as Zeke doesn't catch you, you'll be fine."

"Yeah," Willy answered. "That's what I mean. If both of us pull something, Zeke will go easy. He might even get a good laugh. But if it's just me, he'll get mad."

"So," said Chris, "you're just afraid that Zeke will get upset if you pull a trick like that."

"Exactly," Willy replied. "And Zeke can be a real pain when he's on the warpath."

Chris said nothing.

The boys came to the top of a ridge and saw the camp beneath them, in a clearing. Three tents were set up: one for Sam and Pete, another for Chris and Willy, and the third for Zeke.

As they got closer, they saw Zeke hunched over a fire. He looked up as they entered the clearing. "Welcome," Zeke said in his strong baritone voice. "Did you find anything better up the trail?"

"No," said Chris, checking his watch. "I went for exactly half an hour, like you said. But I must have been slower coming back."

"That's fine," Zeke said. "Out here there's no clock to punch. I hope you didn't mind me sending Willy after you. I see he found you."

Chris shot a glance at the younger Washington boy. "Willy? I didn't see Willy, but I did see a bear."

Zeke looked at Chris knowingly, then at Willy, and then said with a chuckle, "A *black* bear no doubt."

Chris chuckled too. "A big *ugly* black bear."

Willy sniffed.

"We went ahead and set up the tents," Zeke went on, changing the subject. "Sam and Pete wanted to sack out for a while before dinner, and after about forty minutes, we figured you hadn't found anyplace better. So grab a piece of ground and kick off your boots."

Chris needed no encouragement. In an instant, he was on the ground by the fire, tugging at a double knot.

It was a great evening—the kind that made all the hiking worthwhile, even for Chris. After Zeke whipped up his Miracle Stew for dinner, he got out his harmonica and they sang all the songs they knew—camp songs, school songs, Sunday school songs. The sky was clearer than any of the Ringers had ever seen. The stars winked at them between the spreading branches of the trees.

Marshmallows came out later, and each of the campers found a stick to roast them on. Then they placed them on chocolate bars between graham crackers. It was a gooey mess, but tasty beyond belief.

Later, each boy told a story.

Willy started by telling a ghost story about a mysterious house with chains rattling and a voice calling, "IT FLOATS!" He had them all spooked until the final line, when they erupted in laughter.

Pete told about a case his father worked on in the FBI. It was a bank robbery ring that they finally hunted down after analyzing the ink used on the holdup notes.

Chris talked about some of his earliest memories, from when his father was alive. There was a day at the beach, when the whole family went to Ocean City, Maryland. Chris remembered getting sand in his eyes and crying, but being picked up by his father and feeling very safe.

Zeke told an old story he had heard on the trail, about a mysterious hiker who helped people in need. The Appalachian Samaritan, he said, seemed to appear out of nowhere and then vanish after doing his good deed.

Sam showed the others his walking stick, a beautifully carved staff that used to belong to his grandfather, Pablo Ramirez, who traveled through the mountains of Mexico, preaching the Bible to anyone who would listen. Sam's father had given Sam the walking stick for this trip.

When all had told their stories, it was late and they

were yawning. They hit the sack and slept soundly,
dreaming of ghosts and girlfriends, fathers and grandfathers.

Turn to page 28.

Hang on, Kenny," said Jim. "If I stay up here, the catwalk might collapse. I'll go for help."

"Don't leave me!" Kenny cried.

"It'll be OK, Kenny. Don't worry. I'll be back soon."

"Don't leave me!"

"I won't leave you. I've gotta go get help. I'll be back. I promise."

Kenny whimpered, but Jim gingerly scrambled down the steps and joined the girls.

"What happened to Kenny? We heard a scream," Tina said.

"He fell," Jim answered, rushing by them. "We have to get help."

Jill started to head into the woods, toward Millersburg. "No," Jim said, "Forest Creek. It's closer."

In fact, there was a road just fifty yards from the water tower, a road that led into the Forest Creek development. Jim flagged down a car. "There's an emergency," he told the driver. "Can you take us to a police station or fire station? We need help."

Fortunately, the driver had a car phone, and he quickly dialed for help. In minutes there was a police car, a fire truck, and an ambulance screaming toward them. Two men in fire gear hopped out. "Someone's stuck on the water tower," Jim called to them.

The firemen swiftly set up the supports for the snorkel truck—a fire truck that has a hydraulic crane with a basket on the end of it—and then one of them jumped into the basket and positioned himself under Kenny. The fireman grabbed Kenny and pulled him into the basket and then lowered the basket safely to the ground. With a word of thanks to Jim and the girls, the firemen left, and the paramedics took Kenny to the hospital for observation. The police stayed behind to question the Ringers about the accident. After they got the answers they needed, the police thanked the Ringers for their quick thinking and left.

"I guess he'll be going home now," sighed Tina.

"If they figure out where he lives," added Jill.

Tina picked up the blanket she had dropped by the fence near the base of the water tower. "I hope he'll be all right."

"We saved him, didn't we?" Jim asked.

Tina looked in the direction the firemen had gone. "Well, sort of."

Tina took the blanket home and washed it. She didn't know where Kenny lived, or who his parents were, or his last name. All she knew about him was what Jim had told her. But her heart ached for Kenny anyway.

Tina folded the blanket gently and placed it at the foot of her own bed. She knelt down and thought of Kenny. "Lord," she prayed, "please take care of Kenny. Don't let him run away again. Somehow, make his parents get back together and love him and love each other. Just make it happen, Lord . . . please . . . for Kenny's sake."

Sometimes you just have to pray as bold a prayer as

108

you possibly can. You're asking for a miracle. You know it shouldn't be able to happen. But you believe in God. You believe, and you just have to pray a bold prayer. That's what Tina prayed. She was just sure God would answer.

She was just sure.

THE END

Turn to page 141.

Look, guys," said Zeke, "we really have to keep going. If we don't get to the shelter by sundown, we may get lost. I know your shoulder's hurting, Sam, but it'll be worse if you have to sleep on the damp ground tonight. Let's go."

So they moved on through the woods, with Zeke leading the way, Chris and Willy walking a few steps behind him, taking turns carrying Sam's backpack, and Pete and Sam walking in the back.

It bothered Pete to see Sam in such pain. Every step made Sam wince.

"Tell me about your dream," said Pete, trying to take Sam's mind off the pain.

"I was in Mexico. It was hot and wet, but I hiked through a jungle and came to a little town. Everyone was very thirsty. There was a huge water tank in the town, but no one knew how to turn on the faucet that sent the water to the houses."

"No one knew how to turn on the faucet?" Pete asked.

"I know it's dumb, but it was a dream. So anyway, I just walked up to the tank and turned on the faucet and suddenly there was water everywhere. People were drinking it and swimming in it. Kids were running around in the sprinklers. It was great—and I was a big hero."

"For turning on the faucet?"

"Yep. But then I turned around, and there was this big wolf. They called him Ray Lobo."

"Who did?"

"The people. They were all around, calling, 'Ray Lobo, Ray Lobo.' They told me he was the king of the wolves. He looked really vicious."

"Like Old Man Foster's Doberman?"

"Worse. He had huge teeth, and they were really sharp. His claws were like nails. And he was twice as big as me. He jumped at me and I ducked. He did not like that at all. He was growling, and everyone said, 'Ray Lobo! Ray Lobo!' and I just wanted to go home."

"Or wake up."

"Right. But I didn't. Not yet. The wolf came at me again and knocked me to the ground. I rolled over on top of it, but it scratched me with its claws and rolled on top of me. That's when it bit me."

"Where?"

"Well, it was going for my neck, but I turned at the last minute, so it got me farther down."

"Like your shoulder?"

Sam stopped walking for a second and looked at his friend in amazement. "That's right! It was my shoulder. The same one that's hurting now. That's weird."

"So what happened then?" Pete asked.

"Well, I bit him back."

"You bit the wolf?"

"Sure. It tasted awful, but it got him off me. Then I punched him in the gut—he howled something awful—and I pinned him."

"So what did he do?"

"I don't know," Sam said. "That's when I woke up."

"Wow!" Pete marveled. "So you were beating the king of the wolves. Cool dream."

"Yeah, better not fight me. I can beat a wolf."

"I know," Pete agreed, "and you might bite."

In front of them, Chris called out, "Guess what, folks! It's raining!"

Pete held his hand in the air. "Yes, it is," he agreed. Then he turned to Sam and teased, "You had to turn on that water, didn't you?"

The rain began to come down hard. Zeke pulled a tarpaulin from his pack, which he draped over Sam, but everyone else was getting drenched.

"Wait," said Chris. "Why don't we just stop here and set up our tents? We're gonna be soaked!"

Zeke gave Chris a frustrated look. "Chris, if we camp out here, we'll be even more miserable. We need to keep moving. A little rain won't hurt us."

CHOICE ➡️

If they put up their tents now, turn to page 11.

If they hurry toward the shelter, turn to page 60.

I've got an idea," said Zeke. "Let's hike with them for one day, and then we'll go and do our own thing. We've still got another week on this trip. We'll have plenty of time with each other."

Chris still wasn't sure, but the others agreed with Zeke's plan.

They set out together the next morning, eight hikers in all—Zeke leading the four Ringers, and Bill leading Bob and young Robby. Bob's jovial spirit kept everyone in a good mood, and Robby enjoyed being with the group. Sam and Pete even tried to learn some sign language so they could "talk" to Robby. Chris and Willy explained to Bob how the Ringers got their name, telling about the old church and the bell in the tower. Bob told about his own church, back in New Jersey, and how special it was to him. Bill kept to himself pretty much, but by the afternoon Zeke managed to get into a conversation with him, asking him about his army days.

The fun continued at dinner and afterward. Bob had all sorts of word games and brain teasers for the group to play. And he told stories the guys could hardly believe—all true, but the kind of story that makes you shake your head in disbelief. He had everyone in stitches with tales of college pranks he had pulled. Even Chris had to admit that he was having more fun than they would be having without the Pressers. The group's laughter filled the woods.

The shelter that night was a bit small, so Zeke and Bill each set up a pup tent in the clearing. After they all said their good-nights, they went to bed.

All the talk about pranks got Willy and Chris whispering together. Staying awake until everyone else was asleep, they slipped out of bed and walked into the clearing where the two pup tents were set up. Willy showed Chris how to loosen the tent pegs so that when Zeke stirred in the morning, his tent would fall in on him. Then, giggling, they went back to bed.

Willy was a light sleeper anyway, so he awoke with the dawn and nudged Chris. Then they watched Zeke's tent and waited. He was usually the first one up, so they prepared for a big laugh. But there was still no movement from the tent. When the others in the shelter started to wake up, Willy decided to hurry things along. He walked out into the clearing and called toward the tent. "Zeke!"

"Yes," Zeke said, stepping out from behind the shelter and surprising Willy. He wasn't in the tent at all. "What did you want, Will?"

There was a grunt from the tent and some movement. Willy looked back at Zeke, puzzled. *If Zeke is here, then who is in the—?*

The tent shook, the pegs came loose, and it fell in. Chris, watching from his bunk, started laughing. "Ha, Zeke! We got you now!"

"Oh, really?" said Zeke, stepping in front of the shelter, much to Chris's surprise.

Bill Presser crawled out of the collapsed tent and glared up at the others. Stepping toward Willy and towering above him, Bill belted out, *"YOU!* DID YOU DO THIS?"

"Yes, s-s-sir," Willy whimpered. "I did." He cringed, fearing what the huge, angry person would do.

Suddenly Willy heard a hearty laugh behind him. It was Bob.

"Did you see that?" Bob chortled. "That was great! I wish I had thought of that. That was so funny, Bill, to see you crawling out of your tent like that. You didn't know what hit you!"

Bill's look softened.

"And what's so great," Bob went on, "is that the kid was trying to do it to his brother! He got the wrong tent! He got my brother instead!" Again he erupted into fits of laughter.

Bill began to smile. "Yeah," he said. "I guess that is pretty funny."

"Good thing for you it wasn't *me* in there," Zeke told his kid brother. "I'd be wasting your face in the woods right now."

It was Chris who asked the Pressers if they'd join the Ringers for one more day of hiking. But after that, Bob and Robby and Bill had to go home.

Willy never forgot the surprise and fear and joy of that failed prank.

THE END

Turn to page 141.

This is our trip," Willy said. "Solo."

"Yeah," Chris agreed. "It's bad enough that we have to share the shelter with them, but let's have our own campfire."

Zeke explained that they couldn't really build another fire. The cinder blocks that were set up there—that was really the only safe place to start a fire, and the other group had already claimed it.

"Well, maybe we can just go to bed early," said Chris.

"Yeah," said Willy, "we can tell ghost stories in our bunks."

Sam and Pete really didn't care, so Zeke lost this vote, two to one. They decided to share the fire to cook their dinner, and then to retreat to their bunks.

It was an awkward evening. The Pressers stayed around the fire until late. Chris and Willy swapped ghost stories for a while, but then they began to retell old ones until they were bored. Pete scratched notes on a new design for the computer he was building back home. Sam just wanted some rest. Zeke hung out that night with the Presser family around the campfire and had a good time getting to know them.

The awkwardness continued into the next morning, as both groups had separate breakfasts in the cramped space that was available. The Pressers hit the trail first, pulling on their backpacks and disappearing down the hill.

The Ringers watched them go.

"Did you guys enjoy your 'solo' evening?" asked Zeke.

"Eyah," said Sam with a look of distaste, "it was all right. I think you had more fun gabbing with those Prestones all night."

Zeke nodded. "You guys would have enjoyed 'em."

"Who were they?" asked Pete.

Zeke opened his mouth to say something, but stopped himself and just smiled.

"Oh, come on!" all four said at once.

"If you really wanted to know, you could have talked with them yourself. You had last night and this morning."

The guys all cried foul, but Zeke stood firm. "I'm not going to be your source of cheap gossip!"

"We don't want you to gossip, Kimosabe, we just want you to tell us about your friends." Sam tried to sound sincere.

Zeke saw through it. "Like I said," the older, wiser of the five repeated, "if you really wanted to know who the Pressers were, you could've talked with them yourself. But I'm *not* your personal spy."

"You're not?" Sam said, looking disappointed.

Zeke rolled his eyes.

"We could catch up with them!" suggested Willy, as if he had had a brilliant idea.

Pete slapped his forehead in disbelief. "Willy, you'll try *anything.*"

"Come on! Come on!" Willy picked up his pack and

started hiking. The others looked at each other until finally they all just went along.

They knew they would have to hike at quite a clip to catch up with the "Prestones," as Sam kept calling them. They got into it, though, by pretending to be in a race. Willy had the lead until Sam took it. Pete snuck past Sam on an inside-lane maneuver. But his lead lasted only seconds, when Chris, a little less willing than the others to be in anything but first place, took it from Pete and held off the others with tactical elbow jabs. Finally, Willy came up from behind and convinced Chris to form a "salt and pepper" moving roadblock with him to fend off the others. They held the lead as a pair until the Pressers came into view up ahead.

When the checkered flag finally flew, the whole gang of four had a massive pileup right in front of the Pressers . . . to Zeke's equally massive embarrassment.

Zeke's high-performance Ringers hiked the rest of that day with the strangers they had scorned the night before. They had a great time together. And then the two groups parted ways.

Zeke was right. They enjoyed 'em.

THE END

If you haven't come across Kenny and his adventures yet, turn to page 45 and make different choices along the way.

Or, turn to page 141.

Zeke turned toward them, still in his sleeping bag, and propped himself up on an elbow. "Are you sure this is what you heard? You weren't dreaming?"

"We both heard it," Pete said.

"How many men were there?"

Sam tried to remember. "Three, I think. Maybe four."

"Well, if there are three," Zeke said, "we may be able to take them."

"Take them?" gulped Chris.

"Capture them. Detain them," Zeke explained. "We could tie them up with tent rope and go for help. But if there are four, that's a problem."

"There are five of us," Willy chirped.

"Four-and-a-half," Sam corrected. "And they're men. We're just kids."

"We could use the element of surprise," Zeke said.

"How?" Chris wondered.

Zeke thought for a moment. "Ever read the story of Gideon in the Bible? Sudden light, sudden sound, they're scared silly."

"Yeah," Chris muttered. "But we're not Gideon."

"I think we ought to go for help," Willy said.

Zeke considered this, too. "You may be right."

"How?" asked Pete. "We can't exactly go to the nearest tree and dial 9-1-1."

Zeke reminded them of the road they crossed that day. There was a ranger station near that crossing. It was probably a two-hour walk, and it might be dangerous at night.

"Can't be any more dangerous than staying here with a team of terrorists next door, can it?" Willy asked.

"Wait!" said Pete. "I have an idea! We could throw a tarp over them. We have this tarp, right? With holes at the edges for rope, right? So we thread the rope all around it and throw the tarp over them as they're sleeping. They wake up, try to struggle free, but we pull the rope tight and bag them."

"A bag of terrorists," Sam said. "I like it."

"What if they have guns?" Zeke asked.

Pete scratched his chin. "I hadn't thought of that."

Everyone thought for a moment. "I think we can take them," Zeke said finally. "If we went for help, they'd be gone by the time we got back. It's obvious that they need to be stopped, and I think we can do it."

They decided to use Pete's plan: a tarp with ropes threaded through it. Surprise the terrorists and capture them, tie them up, and then go for help.

Sam was sent as a spy to see if they were sleeping yet. He crept to the place and listened. He heard nothing. *Maybe they've gone away!* But then he heard the sound of breathing, the heavy sighing of sleep. He shined a dim flashlight on them and learned that there were three men, all lying down, asleep. Some packs, which probably held their guns, if they had them, were off to the side. *Perfect!*

Returning to camp, Sam gave his report and then led the others into position. Just as Zeke was about to throw the tarp, Sam slid on a slippery spot of ground and gave a yelp.

That ruined everything. One of the men awoke and scrambled out of his sleeping bag. Chris and Willy turned on their flashlights, but Zeke was slow in throwing the tarp. The other men were awakened by the noise, and by the time the tarp came down on them, they easily threw it off. One man grabbed Chris and threw him to the ground. When Willy went to help, he too was thrown down. Chris and Willy were quickly tied together with their own rope. A second man went after Pete and a third corralled Zeke. Sam was still down from the original slip, and he was too stunned to move.

Soon all five hikers were tied up in the middle of this small clearing. The man with a deep voice shined a flashlight in their eyes and asked them questions. The other two waved guns around—big guns, automatic weapons that ordinary mortals saw only in movies.

Zeke and the others explained, over and over, that they were just hikers, but these ruffians seemed unmoved.

"Let's get out of here," one man said.

"No!" another said. "They've seen us. They've gotta die!"

The third turned and looked Zeke in the face. He thought for a second, chewing something, his bad breath wafting over Zeke's frightened face. He scowled, then held the muzzle of his gun to Zeke's head.

"Bye-bye," he said calmly.
"NOOOOOOO!" Sam screamed.

Turn to page 67.

122

Jim had second thoughts, but decided to go along with what Jill said. *She's an adult. She can take care of herself,* he decided.

The three went into the Freeze for Mr. Weatherly's Coke. When they came out, the woman was still sitting on the pavement, obviously in pain. Mrs. Williams, who worked at the bank, was coming down the street. *Maybe she'll offer to help,* Jim thought.

After delivering the Coke to Mr. Weatherly, the three hikers continued their tour of the Common but soon got bored with it. They walked by all the shops that bordered the Common, but they already knew most of those. By about four o'clock, they were getting bored and cranky and decided to call it a day.

THE END

If you haven't found out what reward Jill, Jim, and Tina receive, turn to page 57 and make different choices along the way.

Or, turn to page 141.

Chris spoke up. "We were trying to scare them. It was a joke. We thought it would be funny."

Zeke shook his head and kicked at the ground. "It was so funny that you nearly got your head bashed in. It's a good thing Pete had the sense to come and get me. And Sam, cut the cowabunga stuff, OK? If you've got a problem, tell me. I'll take care of it.

"Now, we're going to need some more firewood for tonight. Go find some, but don't go far; it's almost dark."

They scattered and searched the ground for usable branches. Willy sidled up to Chris and said, "Thanks, buddy."

"What for?"

"For sharing the blame with me. I got you into this. You could have just blamed me."

Chris smiled. "Yeah, but I went along with it. And what are friends for?"

"Well," Willy answered, "Zeke would have killed me if it was all my fault. I owe you one."

"*Two*," Chris corrected. "You owe me at least two."

The mood was strained that evening. Everyone was still in shock over the near accident, and Zeke was grumpy. They roasted a few marshmallows, and Chris's kept falling into the fire. He did get his boots off, finally.

All five took to their tents pretty early. It had been a

full day. The campers dreamed of Millersburg, their home, their families, schoolmates, and the other Ringers who couldn't make this trip.

All but Sam, that is. Sam dreamed of Mexico's mountains. He saw himself traipsing those trails with the great Pablo—missionary hiker, explorer, wolf hunter.

Turn to page 28.

This time Tina voted with Jim, and the three Ringers set off through the woods toward Forest Creek. Jim carried the cat in his arms. Midnight was completely black except for a bit of white on her ear and tail.

"I hope this cat doesn't give us bad luck," Jill groused.

"Oh, I'm not superstitious," said Tina. "God is bigger than all that good-luck/bad-luck stuff."

There was no special trail, but the woods were not difficult to cross. In a short time they burst out again into the open sunlight that was shining down on the split-level houses and well-cut lawns of Forest Creek. The first street they came to was Almond, and the second was Beech.

"I bet the next is Cherry," Jim said, and he was right.

They found their way to number 102, with "Moffatt" painted on the mailbox. Tina rang the doorbell.

The door was answered by a large woman with her hair in curlers. She took one look at the cat and cried, "Midnight!" The cat jumped out of Jim's arms and darted into the house.

"So I guess that's your cat," said Jim.

"Yes, indeed," said the woman. "We were so worried. Wherever did you find her?"

Jim told the story of finding the cat in Millersburg and bringing her through the woods.

126

"So you probably want your reward now," the woman said, stepping back in her front hallway.

"There's a reward?" Jill asked in surprise.

"The tag didn't say anything about a reward," Jim mumbled.

The woman handed them an envelope. "Well, here you go. Thanks again ever so much."

Inside the envelope were four all-day passes to Wild 'n' Wacky, the hot new amusement park in the next county. "But there are only three of us," Jill exclaimed. "Who should we ask to go with us?"

This little dilemma led to a lively debate about how to choose one of the other Ringers above the rest. Willy? Sam? Pete? Chris? Or even Jess?

Suddenly Jim said, "How about Mr. Weatherly?"

"Yeah!" said the other two. "After all, he's the one who found Midnight."

"Boy, are the guys going to be jealous!"

And so it was decided. And the three took off back toward Millersburg to deliver Mr. Weatherly's reward.

THE END

Turn to page 141.

Sam surprised his attackers by rushing right at them. "Pete!" he cried. "I won't let them get you!"

He managed to knock one down, and he eluded the other. He had reached the man who was holding Pete, and he tried to pry those stubby fingers away. They would not give. Finally, Sam bit the hand, tasting the strong flavor of nicotine. "Yuk!" Sam said, but the hand had moved. Pete was free.

"Run, Pete, run!" Sam yelled. "Get out of here!"

Pete did not move.

"We've gotta zap, man, right away!" Sam pleaded, but Pete stayed perfectly still.

Suddenly the light was shining in Sam's eyes. An eerie voice said, "Here's the one we want, the one who wrestles with wolves."

Pete's hands were on Sam's shoulders. It was reassuring at first, but then Pete started to clench the shoulders tighter and tighter. Sam was stunned to hear Pete say, "Here he is, gentlemen. I said I would get him for you."

Turn to page 67.

Pete took off his glasses and tried to wipe them with his shirttail. He looked around at the three blurry figures of his friends and at Zeke, who was taller but also blurry. Then he looked over at the blurry men standing by the fire and the vague outline of the kid staring into the woods. *From this view, we're all the same,* he noticed.

"Come on, Chris," said Pete. "Don't be so antisocial. We can have fun with them, too."

"Yeah," said Sam.

"I agree," Willy proclaimed, after giving Pete's suggestion some thought.

Chris just shrugged. He was outvoted.

Zeke walked back to the fire with a cheerful grin. "We'd be happy to join you for dinner," he said. "What can we do to help?"

Bob looked around. "Nothing that I can see. You might as well just claim your bunks and set up your bedrolls. What are you eating?"

"Just MRE's," Zeke answered.

"Ah yes," Bob chuckled. "Meals Ready-to-Eat." He reached inside a backpack he had beside him and pulled out a metallic-looking packet. "We've got 'em, too."

Zeke tried to read the label. "What's that? Chicken Teriyaki?"

"It's amazing what they're doing with freeze-dried

food these days," laughed Bob's brother, Bill. "Nothing like when I was in the army."

Just then Pete came up to join the conversation. "You were in the army?"

Bill nodded. "Vietnam."

"Cool," said Pete.

Bill shook his head. "No, not cool. *Interesting*. Always interesting. Never cool."

"How's your water supply?" Bob interrupted. He went on to suggest that a few hikers go to a stream they had found about a quarter mile away. They could fill up their canteens and water pouches and get some extra water for washing the dinner utensils.

Pete volunteered, but the other Ringers were too bushed. Bob decided to go himself and to bring his son, Robby. So Pete gathered up all the Ringers' canteens and set off with Bob. Instead of calling young Robby, Bob went and put his hand on Robby's shoulder. The boy seemed jolted from his trance, but he cheerfully went along. Robby looked about ten or eleven, with short red hair and a few freckles. He seemed to be a happy kid, but he kept quiet.

"What a great place this is!" exclaimed Bob as they began walking.

"Yes," said Pete. He decided he liked this jolly man, though he wasn't sure exactly why. Normally, people who were too friendly turned him off. But there was something real about Bob.

"It just fills my heart with such appreciation for our Creator," Bob went on. Pete noticed that Bob was moving his fingers rapidly as he talked. Bob saw something fly between a pair of trees. He pointed, crouching down to get a good view.

"Look!" he whispered. There was a beautiful blue bird sitting on a branch. Bob moved his hands quickly in front of Robby, and Robby moved his own hands in response. Pete was fascinated by this conversation the father and son were having.

The bird flew off and Bob stood up. "I was just telling Robby th—," Bob began, but then he noticed the amazed look on Pete's face. "Oh, I didn't tell you. My son is deaf. But we do just fine, talking with our hands." He was signing with his hands again, for Robby's benefit. "Right, Rob?"

Robby smiled and gave a thumbs-up sign.

"I think that's great," Pete said. "I mean, the way you do that."

"Thank you," Bob said. Even now, as they walked, Bob was signing the words to Robby. "Robby's a smart kid, even though he can't hear. And he says a lot of clever things."

Robby made a few hand motions, and Bob let out a hearty laugh. "You know what he said? 'Aw, shucks!'"

They reached the stream, which was coursing through a narrow ravine, and filled their canteens. In sign language, Robby asked if he could go wading. Bob checked his watch and nodded, and in moments Robby had his shoes and socks off. Pete sat with Bob at the entrance of the ravine.

"It must be difficult sometimes," Pete said, nodding in Robby's direction.

"It was at first," Bob said candidly. "My wife and I were

pretty upset when Robby was born like that. But we prayed a lot about it, and God gave us a real peace."

Pete was pleased to hear someone else talk about God. "Are you a Christian?"

"Why yes, I am," Bob answered. "Are you?"

"Yes," Pete said. "But I'm still learning."

Another jolly laugh from Bob. "Aren't we all?"

On their way back, Bob, Pete, and Robby talked about the beauty of the trail. "Sometimes," Bob said, "being a Christian is like hiking through the wilderness." Pete liked that. He didn't know it right then, but he would remember that comment for a long time.

The campfire that night was great. Bob dug out some marshmallows for roasting, and they sang songs and told stories well into the night.

Just before they hit the sack, Bob said, "It's been great to get to know you tonight. It's always fun to meet other hikers, especially those who love the Lord. I was wondering if you guys would like to join us in our hike tomorrow. We're going the same direction, and it would be great to spend more time with you."

"That's very nice," said Zeke, "but—"

"Look," Bob added, "I don't want to pressure you. You may want to spend more time getting to know each other. That's fine. You can say no if you want. Our feelings won't be hurt. But I just thought—well, my boy really likes you guys. He doesn't have many friends back home, and it's been really good for him to meet you. Hey, I'll let you talk about it."

With that, Bob stood and walked to the shelter where

132

Robby was already sleeping. Bill followed him so the Ringers could discuss the matter in private.

"They're a lot of fun," said Pete. "Let's do it."

"But this wasn't what we planned," Chris countered. "Nothing against them, but it's more relaxing when it's just us, don't you think?"

CHOICE ⇒

If they decide to hike with the others, turn to page 112.

If they decide not to, turn to page 51.

Why don't we just see if this woman is all right. If she isn't, I'm sure Mr. Weatherly will understand," said Jim as he crossed the street. Jill and Tina followed him.

"Are you all right, ma'am?" Jim asked.

She looked up, squinting in the sun, and shook her head while biting her lip. She had been crying so hard that her eye makeup was streaming down her face along with her tears.

"What's wrong?" Tina said softly, coming closer.

"Oh, nothing," she said through her tears.

Jim was surprised at the woman's answer, since her shoe was obviously in two pieces. They were the high-heeled kind, too, so that she couldn't exactly wear one without the other.

"Is there anything we can do to help?" Jim asked again. "You know, there's a shoemaker in town who can fix that shoe for you in a jiffy—"

"It's not the shoe!" the woman wailed.

Tina looked with compassion at the miserable young woman and said, "You're having a bad day, aren't you?"

"YE-E-E-E-SSSS!" she wailed. "I was having lunch with my boyfriend today because it's his birthday. So I got out of work an hour early so I could buy him a present. But I had this big fight with my boss before I left work, so I don't know if I still have a job when I get back. So I went to this nice store down here to buy my boyfriend a shirt, and I didn't like anything there. But I had to get him *something,* so I just grabbed something, and I was still late for lunch. But that was OK because my boyfriend was in a bad mood, and he broke up with me right before dessert, so I left and decided to take back the shirt. But I lost the receipt, so they wouldn't take it back. So I'm stuck with this lousy shirt and no boyfriend and maybe no job, and my heel just fell off!" The woman tried to wipe her nose as delicately as possible, but she didn't have any tissue. Jim reached into his pocket and pulled out a Brazilian bandana he sometimes carried with him and offered it to her. She took it and blew her nose.

"I know what you need," said Jill, confidently. "Dessert!"

The woman laughed through her tears. The others did, too. Together they convinced the woman to come into the Freeze with them and have one of Jill's ice-cream sundae designs.

"Do you like chocolate?" Jill asked.

"Yes!" the woman answered.

"Then it's a Triple Chocolate Sundae Supreme you need," she announced. She whipped up her best ever and brought it to the table. "If this won't make you forget your troubles, nothing will."

The kids introduced the woman—Suzanne was her name—to Betty. Betty said she knew the owner of the clothing store and would see if she could return the shirt. As it turned out, Betty's husband did a lot of business with the company Suzanne worked for; he could put in a good word for her. And as for the boyfriend, well, Betty said she knew lots of eligible young men.

"Oh no!" Jill said. "I forgot Mr. Weatherly's Coke!" She took a paper cup from behind the counter and filled it with ice and Coke, as Betty had taught her to. Then the three Ringers said good-bye to Suzanne and went back to deliver the drink to Mr. Weatherly.

They found him patiently waiting. A cat had settled in his lap, and he was absentmindedly petting it. "Sorry, Mr. Weatherly, but we had a little interruption."

"No matter," said the elderly man.

"I see you have company," said Tina, with a nod toward the cat.

"Yes, this is Midnight," Mr. Weatherly said. "At least that's what the tag says. Midnight seems to be lost, or else she's mighty far from home."

They checked the tag. It said: IF LOST, RETURN TO THE MOFFATTS, 102 West Cherry, Forest Creek, VA.

"If I had a car, I'd drive her over there," said Mr. Weatherly. "But I don't drive anymore."

"We can walk it," Jim exclaimed.

"You just want to hike through those woods," Jill charged.

"That's probably the fastest way," Jim replied. "Come on, we can do a good deed and have fun, too."

"And get all scratched up along the way!" Jill countered. "Haven't we done enough good deeds today?"

136

CHOICE ⇉

If they return the cat, turn to page 125.

If they don't, turn to page 13.

Have a good one," Willy called out to the deer as it vanished into the woods. "I've gotta zap."

The deer probably didn't know what "zapping" was, especially since the Ringers had just started using the term a few weeks earlier. If you have to leave, like, right away, then you've gotta zap. Willy had to zap back to camp and get more wood along the way. The deer had its own reason to zap.

By the time Willy got back to the shelter, the others had unpacked some gear and were ready to start preparing dinner. Zeke took the branches from Willy and carefully placed them in the concrete-block grill. He spread out some kindling that Sam and Pete had gathered and put another branch over it. Then he took a match from his pocket and lit the kindling, blowing lightly on it until the flame got going.

"If your brother's such a great camper," Chris asked Willy, "why doesn't he just rub two sticks together?"

"He's so good, he only needs one," Willy replied. "A matchstick."

It was a good evening. For dinner, they opened vacuum-packed pouches of ready-to-eat meals, which they added boiling water to. It wasn't home cooking, but they had fun complaining about it. All five hikers were tired from the hiking, but it was a good kind of tired.

The fire was dying down to glowing embers, and the hikers sat around it. The night had brought a slight chill, and each one of the campers had put on a sweatshirt.

"If you weren't here," Chris asked the group, "where would you want to be?"

Each one answered differently. Sam said he'd want to be visiting his Aunt Stella and Uncle Morris. "You wouldn't believe the great time we have together."

Pete said he'd want to be at home working on a new project. He was building his own computer.

Willy said he'd like to be at the Freeze enjoying a butterscotch sundae, instead of this "beef Stroganoff in a pouch."

Chris said he'd want to be at the old church in Millersburg. "It may sound funny, but I like being there. When I'm there, I feel like God is real close."

"What about you, Zeke?" Chris prodded. "Where would you want to be?"

Zeke just smiled. "Oh, I don't know."

Willy recognized that smile. "He'd want to be with *Brianna*."

The other three boys all chorused, "Brianna?"

"Quiet, Will," Zeke said sternly—but with a smile.

"Yes, folks," Willy continued, "the Zekemeister is in love."

"With *Brianna?*" Chris asked. "It sounds like a laundry detergent."

"Hey!" said Zeke, "don't go making fun of my girlfriend."

"Oooooooo!" said everyone else.

None of the others had ever really had a girlfriend. Oh, there were the occasional crushes and crashes, but they were all quite unattached—and happy to be that way.

"Tell us about her," said Sam. "Is she animal, vegetable, or mineral?"

Zeke had that same silly smile. He was thinking.

"She's gorgeous," Willy piped up. "She's been over to our apartment a lot lately. She's really pretty."

"Well, *I* think she is," Zeke agreed, looking across the campfire at his brother. "But don't be looking for that all the time. People don't—*girls* don't have to be pretty. Look at their *souls*."

Chris looked puzzled. "What do you mean?"

"Well, she's alive. She's the most alive person I've ever known. We talk about a lot of stuff together. It's like she's a friend of mine—and I'm a friend of hers."

"Wow," Sam whispered. He had never heard anyone describe a girlfriend as a *friend*. It sounded . . . different.

"Do you miss her?" asked Willy. "Being out here in the woods?"

Zeke stood up and walked around the outside of their circle. "Yes, I do. It's not like we have to be together all the time. But it's so nice out here—I wish I could share all this with her."

For a few seconds, no one spoke. Then Willy broke the mood: "She's probably glad to get rid of you for a while."

Zeke threw a marshmallow at him. Willy blocked it, it flew into the air, and he caught it right before it plunged into the fire. Everyone *oooooh*ed.

"Is she a Christian?" asked Chris.

140

Zeke and Willy both nodded, and then Willy's voice strained through the marshmallow in his mouth—the one Zeke had just thrown at him—to answer before his brother could speak, "Sheze moe sprchul un *Eke* is, 'at's or ure!"

This time Zeke ignored him. "Now what do you say we hit the sack? Don't forget to put your shoes up. The porcupines around here will eat right through the leather if they can get to them."

"I still think you're joking about the porcupines," said Sam.

Zeke put up his hands. "Proceed at your own risk, Mr. Ramirez. But if you have to hike barefoot, don't say I didn't warn you."

The hikers took their places on the shelf-bunks in the shelter, placed their shoes on the upper bunks, rolled out their sleeping bags, and crawled in.

Turn to page 82.

Zeke sure is a brave guy, don't you think? Taking four crazy fourteen-year-olds on the Appalachian Trail all by himself. . . . Of course, Zeke *is* Willy's brother. Good thing they get along pretty well, huh?

What other travails await Zeke and his hapless hikers? A personal visit from the Appalachian Samaritan? An ambush on Cuban terrorists? Maybe there's more to the Pressers than meets the eye. What interesting adventures will Jill, Tina, and Jim have hiking around Millersburg? And will the injury to Sam be fatal for all?

If you haven't got answers, go to a page you've already read and make different choices along the way. You'll soon agree with Zeke and the other Ringers—whether you're merely hiking happily in the Blue Ridge Mountains or hanging, with white knuckles, from a water tower, it is "most excellent" to pray!

142

Randy Petersen is a free-lance writer living in New Jersey. He has written youth material for Chapel of the Air and is the author of the book *Giving to the Giver,* also by Tyndale.